Olivia
Enjoy
Romance
always
in love

Chalkboard Romance

Melissa Keir

Chalkboard Romance
Copyright © 2014 Melissa Keir
2nd Edition: 2015

All rights reserved.

5764 Woodbine Ave.
Pinckney, MI 48169

Edited By Nan Sipe
Cover art By Dawné Dominique

DEDICATION

for those who find love where they least expect it...

CHAPTER ONE

Lauren waved goodbye to her last student as he climbed into the backseat of his aunt's car. A sad little guy. Sometimes she wanted to grab Todd and hold him close. He had lost his mother a few months back, and she worried about him. She gave another wave when Todd gazed with soulful eyes out the car window. She never met his dad but hoped someone watched over Todd. Her lips flattened. In her opinion famous reporters don't make good fathers. *At least Todd's dad certainly didn't. Poor child, only the aunt brought him to school or came to his events.*

Heading down the hallway, she straightened her shoulders. "I'll just continue to give Todd as much time and attention I can at school."

Todd's withdrawn nature had affected the other children. Lauren's heart squeezed tight. She understood all about loss. Now that her divorce was final. It was time to move on.

Lauren looked at the nameplate on the classroom door. *Mrs. Fulton.* Someone from custodial would need to change that. She smiled. Maybe after a few dozen reminders she'd get the kids to call her Miss Walsh now. A sigh escaped her lips as she dropped into her desk chair.

"Report cards are done." Coming into her classroom, her co-worker, Melanie Whitman thrust a fist in the air despite the weary set of her shoulders.

"Have you heard back from the dating service yet?"

"Melanie, you're more excited about this date than I am." At her best friend's urging, Lauren had filled out a form for an upscale dating site—The Playhouse. "With spring break, I'd hoped for a break of my own." Another sigh escaped her lips. God she was tired. It took sheer willpower to resist the urge to scrub her hands over her face in hopes of ridding herself of any signs of exhaustion that may be showing. No need to screw up what was left of her makeup. "All I want to do is crawl into bed and sleep."

"Not happening. The dates arranged by the mysterious Master Draikoh San are legendary." Melanie perched on the corner of Lauren's desk. "Supposedly he's arranged for a few Hollywood and Rock 'n' Roll bigwigs. His ability to find the perfect date is astonishing."

Lauren avoided eye contact, pulling papers off her desk. "Since the divorce—Boy, I hate that word—I'm hesitant to jump into the dating scene. I don't want a permanent relationship right now."

"You need to get back on the horse. We talked about this. Someone to soothe your feminine ego would be perfect."

Lauren did want to feel desired and loved again. The Playhouse happened to be hideously overpriced but offered a private select screening with a deep background check on all their clients. Few things were known about the owner of The Playhouse, but Master Draikoh San appeared either part god or part magician but totally reliable, very well respected. He guaranteed his results whether you were looking for a casual affair or long-term love. Most of all, he was discreet.

I'm ready to move forward. She couldn't keep letting her husband's—*ex-husband's*—infidelity overshadow her life.

At least the alimony would go for something good. She took a deep breath. "I'll check my email."

Lauren logged into her account. An email from Master Draikoh was at the top of the list. Her heart began to pound. Nervous to see who Master Draikoh recommended, she hesitated, fingers poised above the keyboard. She agreed to Melanie's demands partially to get her off her back. She pulled her hands back then twisted them. Apprehension, excitement, and determination fought for control.

Teachers aren't seen as hotties except in campy '80s music videos. She shuddered. The video for *Hot For Teacher* crowded her mind. *If I take this step, what will happen to my career? What if someone found out I used a dating service?* Lauren chewed on her lip as she continued to wring her hands anxiously. She threw her shoulders back. *Who am I kidding? The whole process is safe. Besides, I don't care if someone does find out. I deserve this.*

She inched her fingers back toward the keyboard. With a few strokes, she'd find out. Her curiosity would be answered.

"It's here," she said with a whisper. Lauren opened up the email then read the details aloud to Melanie.

"Your night is arranged for next Monday night. I've found the perfect guy for your date. I have included the flight information to Chicago, your room accommodations at the Lotus Hotel, in addition to some details about the man you'll be meeting. Remember our rule…for this first date, only use first names. This enhances your connection. If you want to meet again, you can arrange to exchange numbers afterward. I'm sure you'll have the night you dream of."

Melanie danced around the desk with the news. She looked like one of her students who waited too long to visit the bathroom. Suffice to say, she loved the crazy bitch even when she got on her last nerve or forgot to filter her thoughts. Not even when she failed to escape the lash of her stinging retorts.

"Whoohoo. Chicago. Now tell me the details on your

mystery man. Hopefully he's tall, dark, and handsome with a large package he knows how to use." Melanie laughed. "Hey, you're blushing. What's the deal? I thought you wanted to get laid or at least go have some fun."

Trust Melanie to reduce this romantic date into getting laid. "I do, but I'm not hoping for someone who is rocking in the sack. I'm not looking for a guy who has sex with every girl he meets. I know I signed up for this *perfect date*, but what I really want is someone who will remind me of how special I am. James ruined my self-confidence when he hooked up with that younger bimbo at the office—*The New Mrs. James Fulton.* I feel old, frumpy, unwanted. I need to remember how to love myself again."

"You don't see yourself the way others see you. You have a natural beauty I wish I had. Your complexion has a peach glow and the perfect smattering of freckles. Your brown hair always falls in soft waves. Life isn't fair, God gave you a small waist with sexy long legs."

"Yea, okay." A pout formed on Melanie's face as she looked at her. "What?"

"James really did do a number on your self-esteem," she chided. "I'm sure the guy Master Draikoh picked out will remind you exactly how desirable you are."

"Well, I won't be able to go unless I get some work done here. I hate to leave a mess or have no lessons for when I come back. So, you'd better let me get working or else it'll be your fault I miss this opportunity," Lauren said with a smile.

"I wouldn't want to be the reason behind your bitchy attitude if you don't get your night of passion," Melanie sang out as she headed for the door. "Hey, something just occurred to me," she said, turning back around. "You are so wrong if you're thinking about going on this date in your school clothes and granny panties, we're going to have to hit the Sexy Night store before you leave."

Lauren groaned mournfully, plopping her head in her hands. Melanie had a penchant for tight dresses and expensive shoes, both not her style. Could she even afford to shop with Melanie? The woman's budget made her own look like a pauper's. Mentally, she ran through her closet, dismissing all of her options right away. "Okay," she grudgingly muttered, and frowned at the smirk on Mel's face. "Granny panties and paisley teacher dresses are so not sexy. You're right. But, shopping with you will be torture."

* * * *

After a glass of wine following dinner at the local Italian restaurant, Lauren followed Melanie to the clothing store. The wine helped loosen her up, or at the least, helped make the thought of shopping with her friend tolerable.

The smell of perfume assaulted their senses when they opened the doors. The salesgirl called out.

"Hello, Melanie."

Lauren turned to see a blonde salesgirl in a tight pink minidress waving at them.

"I've got the best new outfits for you. I've been saving them in your size. I had a feeling you'd be in today."

"They know me here," Melanie explained, winking at Lauren. "I spend a fortune in this store. I'm their favorite person." She turned back to the blonde. "Sorry, Cherri. We're here for my friend tonight. She's got a hot date and needs some *get laid* clothes. You know what'll work. Work your magic on her." Melanie pushed Lauren toward Cherri.

When her friend shoved her at Cherri, Lauren couldn't help but notice how thin and perky the girl was. There went her self-esteem, straight in the toilet. No matter what she may try on, nothing was going to look good on her now. Maybe she should make an excuse and leave.

"Don't even think it," Meliane said, guessing her thoughts.

She allowed her friend to drag her back toward the dressing rooms while poor Cherri followed with gigantic piles of clothing and undergarments. Thank goodness they were currently the only customers in the place, there was no way she would parade in front of others in what they will make her try on.

After a while she had to admit the two women had a certain high-class taste for suggestive yet sensual clothing. Ten or more outfits later, her nervousness faded. She was starting to look at this as an adventure. Mel as well as Cherri voiced their opinions on different outfits. Some of their comments shocking her, while others had her laughing outright. Quite a few times, Melanie needed to rush in to help Lauren with the intricacies of some of the attire. One dress happened to be mostly straps which strategically covered only the naughty bits.

"A no way on this one," she called out, "I want my body to look sexy, not red from all the rubbing."

A variety of little black dresses slipped on and off her body in a matter of moments. Flaws with each of them. "I don't know black isn't the best color for me. It makes me look washed-out. Let's try some other colors."

Cherri quickly selected more dresses, bustiers, thigh-high stockings, and barely-there thongs. Trying each on, Lauren felt like a live Barbie doll. They'd pick out the clothes. She'd try them on then parade for their approval. None of the outfits screamed *the one* yet.

A blue jersey dress with a sweeping hemline caught Lauren's gaze. "If I need help getting into these here, who's going to help me get dressed in Chicago?" Lauren shouted. She pulled the blue dress over her head. The fabric hugged her figure. The uneven hemline made her legs look even longer. *Hmm. This one isn't bad.* Lauren twirled in the mirror to get the full effect. She ran her hands over her waist then down her hips, feeling the silky fabric under her hands. The dress hugged her curves, making her feel sexy. She opened the curtain with a flourish.

"Oh wow!"

Lauren smiled at Melanie's encouraging reaction.

"Your date will be helping you out of that dress! Damn girl. You look so good. The neckline shows off your *girls* and the blue makes your eyes seem bigger, too. This dress is a keeper. This guy is definitely going to want to strip you and eat you alive when he sees you."

The pile of clothes to try on dwindled down to nothing while the pile of keepers grew exponentially. The black dresses lay discarded along with the strap number. The corsets and bustiers—also no-gos. Those outfits made her feel like a dominatrix—way outside her comfort zone. The black widow corset she'd tried on only made Cherri and Melanie laugh before suggesting they buy her a whip.

So many of the outfits were wrong for one reason or another. Mainly Lauren felt awkward in them, which defeated the sexiness. The blue dress sat in the keeper pile, along with a sexy baby-blue bra-and-panty set, three sets of thigh-high stockings, along with a short animal-print nightie. A white babydoll nightie with sparkles on the push-up cups rested also in the *yes* category. Three more dresses in greens and prints rounded out what she intended to buy. Each outfit looked tasteful yet fierce. She could well imagine the smoldering look in her date's eyes.

Lauren glanced at the price tags on the keepers. Her stomach tightened. Between the date and the clothes, this adventure was turning into an expensive one. Luckily, she had the money from the divorce. This splurge would be her last. She needed to prove something to herself. She wasn't the person James made her out to be. *Boring Lauren is gone for good. Now there's a new and improved sexy Lauren.*

"Melanie, I can't take all these things for a one-night date," Lauren sassed. "I'd have to change clothes every five minutes just for him to see me in half of these."

Melanie had an answer to that, she always had an answer. To everything. "You, girl, seriously need some new things. Maybe this night will ease you into getting back out in the dating scene enough that you'll definitely need all these racy clothes."

They left the store with three big bags and a huge hug from Cherri. Obviously they had just made the store's monthly numbers. Lauren felt the heat from her credit-card workout through her handbag. Would a credit card melt if you swipe it too much in a short amount of time?

After saying goodbye to Melanie with a promise to call her after her trip, she headed home.

Lauren arrived back at her apartment, placed the bags from Sexy Night on the couch then opened the email from The Playhouse again. She wrote down the details in her calendar with precision and organization that showed in her classroom every day. A sigh escaped her lips as her mind returned to the man she would meet. She queued up the file on her mystery date.

Unfortunately the email included very little information other than his picture and a first name. *Mac. Mac.* His name echoed in her mind. *Mac's a strong, sexy name. It fits his photo. And oh, what a picture.* Her stomach constricted.

He had the appearance of a professional model with those sculpted cheekbones and cleft in his chin. His full mouth looked perfect to feast upon. The tumble of dark hair across his forehead touched her heart. The forelock made her ache to touch him, brush the hair back from his forehead, as she had done a million times for her upset students. Dark stubble graced his face, giving him a dangerous air, making her insides tremble. A hint of playfulness shown on his face, in the unevenness of his smile. Behind the twinkle of his eyes was a glimmer of need. Lauren flushed thinking about those eyes looking at her with desire. She took a deep breath and ran her tongue over her lips to calm herself.

In fact, his eyes seemed familiar to her. Staring at his image, she couldn't place him. If she knew him, she should recognize him. Hating a puzzle, Lauren thought about celebrities, her neighbors, and people from school. Nothing clicked. Her frustration grew, unable to place his face. Maybe he looked like someone else. Besides, it's not like she's going to marry the guy. They were going on *one* date. All she hoped to get out of this adventure was a wonderful night along with a chance to feel sexy again.

Feeling fatigue catching up with her from work, dinner, and shopping, Lauren shut down the computer then headed off to her bedroom with thoughts of her dream date stamped in her mind.

CHAPTER TWO

Crash.

The white dinner plate fell to the floor and shattered. Mac Thomas ran his hands through his hair, staring at the shards on the kitchen floor before closing his eyes. He bit down on the angry words that fought to spill forth. I'm not going to yell, I'm not going to yell, he repeated over and over in his head. He took a deep breath. Then another.

When Mac finally looked at his son, he noticed the tension in his son's shoulders along with the fear on his face. *Do I really yell all the time? I'd never thought raising a child would be so hard.* Mac reached over and hugged Todd. He felt his son's small body trembling in his arms. Mac whispered, "Plates are replaceable. Don't worry." Todd's tremors subsided. "Why don't you go into the living room? I'll clean up here."

Mac watched Todd leave the room at a gallop. The two of them shared the same shade of hair, but Todd's face was all his mother's. It hurt to look at Todd sometimes because of the choices he had made. His gut always churned over the regrets of the past, but there was nothing he could do about it. If onlys are as useless as horse shoes without a horse. What he did now with Todd is what mattered.

Mac tightened his jaw, determined to do better than he'd done in the past. He bent down and picked up the big shards of stoneware. Then grabbed a towel to wipe up the small pieces. Being a parent is a tough job, he gave his parents a lot of credit for raising two kids.

He had let a lot of his responsibilities fall on his sister's shoulders. Now, he felt weary. His feet carried him to the living room where Todd watched cartoons. He loved his son, but being a parent, especially after years of avoiding it, was difficult.

The death of his wife, Claire, left him grappling with the daily routine plus the idiosyncrasies of his seven-year-old son. Todd seemed to have turned into a klutz overnight. Mac was beginning to wonder if the odd behavior was only a stage or something more?

His chest hurt thinking about all the years he wasted, away from home as a foreign news correspondent. Should haves filled his head. *I should have been home more. I should have tried harder.* He only succeeded in creating World War III with Claire.

Mac stood in the door of the living room and watched his son's face in the light of the television screen. He remembered the first time he'd held Todd in his arms. A smile crossed his face. How could he let hate for one person force him to leave the one person he loves.

Mac reached up to massage the back of his neck. He wanted what every parent does, to know his child is healthy but also happy. A chuckle escaped Mac's lips. Healthy…the boy eats like a herd of horses. Even the pediatrician says he's good there.

Mac ran his hand over his jaw as he thought about his son's education and future. He hadn't met any of his teachers yet. Just like he avoided Claire, he avoided Todd's school. He let his sister take over in that department. *I should grow a pair.* Mac snickered at the vulgar thought.

Time to step up and be a parent.

He walked over, bent down, and gave his son another hug before heading back into the kitchen to continue making dinner. A knock on the door had him pausing midstep as Todd jumped up to answer it.

"Hi, Aunt Sherry," his son greeted at the top of his lungs. Todd's buttons appeared stuck on fast plus loud. "Dad's making breakfast for dinner." Todd gave his aunt a quick hug before running back into the living room.

"Hi, Todd, bye, Todd." Sherry laughed.

Sherry shut the door and headed over to give him a kiss on the cheek.

"Mom and Dad send their love. How are you?"

"I'm fine, long day. I have to be an octopus to take care of my little guy. He has way more energy than a middle-aged guy like me. I can only hope spring break is short enough so he can get back to school and on his routine soon. You know how he is with change," Mac explained. "Will you stay for our breakfast dinner?"

"I'd love to," Sherry said with a smile that didn't reach her eyes. "I also have something to show you."

Mac paused in his cooking to take a closer look at his sister as she sat at the kitchen table. Since Claire's death, fear and loss were constant in his life. He hadn't loved Claire but the thought of something happening to his sister frightened him. He walked over, pulled out a chair, and sat next to her at the kitchen table.

"Everything okay with you? With Mom and Dad?" he asked, watching her pull a piece of paper from her purse.

"We're fine. It's nothing like that."

A sigh escaped his lips. "Okay…then what?"

With a frown marring her face, Sherry quietly spoke. "Mac, you've been alone for so long, even before Claire's death. I hate to see you hurting. You've done an amazing job but deserve more. Mac…." She paused to take a breath before continuing. "You deserve a chance at happiness. Do you remember the dating service I used that led me to meeting and marrying Scott after one date?"

Sherry pushed the paper in front of him. "Well, I've arranged for you to have the same chance. I contacted the guy who set up our date—Master Draikoh San from The Playhouse. He's amazing, some even say magical, and has a knack for finding an ideal match for each of his clients."

Mac blinked at Sherry. What was she thinking? "Dating? Me? Marriage with Claire could have soured anyone on dating." He didn't want to hurt her feelings, but he needed to put a stop to her crazy idea.

"I know you're probably upset with me," Sherry told him. "Master Draikoh emailed to say he's found a match and arranged for your perfect date to occur on Monday night in Chicago. All the details are here in the email. Before you say no, at least take a look at the woman."

She pulled a photo out of her purse and laid it on the table. She silently got up to clean up the toys lying on the floor in the living room.

Mac barely gave the photo a glance as he stood to walk over to the sink. He couldn't do this. He understood what his sister was trying to do, but after being trapped in a marriage with Clare, he couldn't help but think all women are just like her. He looked at Sherry and his sour mood lightened. Her heart was in the right place. Maybe there's one or two good women left.

Mac walked back to the table then reached for the photo. The woman's warm smile drew his gaze. His dead wife hadn't been cut out for warmth or motherhood. She'd wanted the prize of a rich husband.

However, as a journalist, he went into the worst parts of the world to get the story. The Middle East wasn't the place for a wife who loved her linen slacks and Ferragamo shoes. Mac steeled his jaw. He was never falling for another high maintenance woman again. He studied the picture intently and tried to measure this woman against the cold fish he'd married. Her brown hair didn't look like it had seen the inside of a million dollar beauty parlor. She held a more natural beauty that he found relaxing.

A cockeyed smile spanned Mac's face as he thought about the past. Money wasn't important to him. He'd been lucky growing up with two down-to-earth parents who just happened to be billionaire philanthropists. Baffled, he scratched his head. How things went so wrong from childhood to adulthood, he didn't know.

Mac always felt Claire got pregnant on purpose. She wanted his money but not his name. He did the right thing and gave her both only to have Claire refuse to put his last name on Todd's birth certificate. They didn't have a marriage but a business arrangement. He wrangled interviews with world leaders in war-torn countries. Claire lived the lavish lifestyle, which made Hollywood wives take notice.

He looked at the now-crumpled photo in his hand. Flattening it out on the table, he stood to grab a glass of orange juice off the counter. He downed it in one gulp. The strong citrusy taste made the pain of the past that much easier to swallow. He filled the glass again, before sitting back down to stare at the rumpled photo.

Running his hand through his hair, Mac thought about his wife. Claire's tumor cut short her wild lifestyle. She'd refused treatment. Didn't want to fight. So she spent her son's early years shopping and spending his money. Her death six months ago brought him back from those poverty-stricken countries to face an even more frightening prospect, his own son. Mac finished the orange juice, picked up the wrinkled photo, and threw it in the garbage.

After dinner with his son and sister and putting Todd to bed, he ended up fishing the photo out of the trash and looking over the info Sherry left on the *date*. Other than her picture, only her first name appeared in the paperwork.

He pulled up information on the computer about The Playhouse Dating Agency and Master Draikoh San. The investigative journalist in him sprung to the surface. He only found glowing praise for this mysterious man from Boynton Beach, Florida. Even his normally skeptical beliefs couldn't find anything shady about this guy or his service. Picking up the phone, he called Sherri.

"All right, I'll do it. Lord knows my life hasn't been normal for a long time. It would make a good story. I don't really know why I changed my mind. Just a gut instinct. I learned in Iraq to go with those. Who's going to watch Todd?"

He had to pull the phone away from his ear at his sister's girlish squeal of delight.

"I'll watch him. You don't have to worry. Since I arranged this whole thing, it's the least I can do."

"The least you can do...I'm scared, Sher. You know what Claire put us through. The fighting. How she threatened to keep Todd from Mom and Dad or you if I ever spoke about divorce. So, I stayed away. Leaving seemed better for everyone." Mac sighed, hating the lump that made his voice tremble as he continued. "What if this woman is like Claire?"

"Mac, this is a date, not a marriage. I know Draikoh has created some wonderful marriages—including my own—but there will be time for weddings later. I want you to find yourself again. I think you desperately need this. You have to heal from the pain your wife put on you. Besides, you can't keep hiding from women because of Claire."

"I'm not hiding from women. I spoke with Mrs. Johnson at the grocery yesterday."

"Be serious, Mac. I can't keep taking Todd to school or meeting with his teachers. You have to man up. Women don't bite unless you want them to."

He could hear the laughter in Sherry's voice. "I understand, Sher. Trusting again...you know how hard it is."

"I do, bro, but Todd's looking to you. I firmly believe this awkward stage is because he's afraid you're going to leave again. He loves you and needs you."

"How did you get so wise? At least Todd got to grow up with the love of you all. Thanks for thinking of me—for being there for us. I love you, Sher."

"Anytime, Mac. I'll see you on Sunday night, so you can get up and get to the airport on time. Night."

After hanging up the phone, he sat looking out the window of his home. Two fawns walked across the lawn. A larger deer joined them. Probably their mother, Mac thought.

Sherry was right. I do need to heal. Maybe learning to trust will make me a better parent. He smiled.

CHAPTER THREE

Lauren's nervousness grew with each step toward the door of the hotel. She toyed with the clasp of her purse as her steps slowed. *Am I really doing this? I can leave right now. No one but me would be wiser.* Her thoughts went round and round about the decision she'd made. Safe Lauren, Boring Lauren were two of the many names James had called her that kept running through her mind. She raised her chin a notch. James's charming personality had swept her off her feet in college. He'd cherished her quirky style yet laid-back attitude. They'd married after college. Things had changed when he got hired at Smithingtons Incorporated. He complained about her hair, the clothes she wore, her figure. His negative words ground her self-esteem into the ground under his feet. She ran her hands down her hips, smoothing the dress. James didn't believe she could be classy enough to be the wife of a rising executive of a big corporation. Well, he's not going to win. Throwing her shoulders back, Lauren resumed walking toward the hotel's door.

Catching the reflected image of a beautiful woman who resembled Jennifer Aniston in the mirrored glass doors, Lauren turned her head quickly to see if she could spot her favorite star. The reflection moved as well. *Oh no, that can't be.* Lauren stepped closer to the window. *The wistful-looking star with long sexy legs in the blue dress...That's me.* Running her hand down her hair, she smiled and felt alive, all tingly yet powerful. Her smile widened. *Maybe, just maybe I can do this.* She held her head high and gave her reflection a little thumbs-up before walking through the door of the hotel.

Lauren glanced around the luxurious lobby. *What a beautiful hotel. So posh.* She made her way toward the concierge desk and the young lady behind the counter.

"Hello, I'm Lauren Walsh. I have a reservation."

The smiling young woman tapped a few keys on her keyboard. "Hello, Miss Walsh. I'm Catherine. I'm happy to help you today. We have your reservation right here. Your two-room suite is 743. It has a magnificent view of Lake Michigan. Your date has checked in already. He's down in the hotel bar and wondered if you wanted to join him there." Catherine handed over a colorful pamphlet.

A blush crept up her face as she took a peek at the key on the inside pocket. She remembered her vow to not let James's evil words win and smiled at Catherine. "Thank you. I'll head to the bar."

"Have you been to Chicago before?"

Lauren shook her head.

Catherine continued, "There's a listing of different events as well as interesting sites in your suite. The bar in your room has anything you might want. Master Draikoh arranged for everything. I'm sure you will find our hotel to be exquisite and lavish. It's the finest one in Chicago. Remember to only use first names for this first date. If you or your date need anything, please let us know. We're always happy to help special friends of Master Draikoh. He's made so many of us happy finding our perfect match. Even our owner found his wife through The Playhouse. Let me grab your bag. I'll have it sent to your room."

With nothing standing in her way, Lauren took a deep breath, put a smile on her face then strode into the bar.

The right heel of her expensive shoes chose that moment to break, tossing her flat on her face.

* * * *

Mac sat at the beautiful mahogany bar nursing his first beer. *I'm more nervous than a long-tailed cat in a rocking chair factory.* The last place he belonged was somewhere as opulent as this. He ran his fingers up and down the condensation on the beer glass. Even though he grew up in a family with a great deal of money, his parents taught him the benefit of working hard and doing what you love. At eighty, his dad still worked in the stables every morning, grooming his horse or was out in the pasture feeding the cattle.

Claire never understood his family. Money wasn't important to them unless the cash could be used to befit someone else. Mac shook his head. Sure, he used his family's money to get inside some of those war-torn countries but only so he could show the world the truth.

He'd worked hard to be impartial but his soft heart swayed him. Seeing any amount of suffering hurt, making him known as a compassionate emissary in those challenging countries.

With Claire gone, his life had changed once again. He took a job as a reporter at the local station affiliate, reporting on the important events happening in his community so he could be at home with Todd. Realizing how much poverty and conflict existed in his own hometown left him cold. They say charity begins at home. Well, he was determined to find a way to help, while setting a good example for his son.

He took a look at the clock on the wall. Where was she? Maybe she took one look at him and ran for the hills.

Mac turned on his barstool in time to see a gorgeous brunette walk into the bar. Her steps seemed to match the beat of his pulse. Shifting in his chair, he adjusted his now-tight, uncomfortable pants. Maybe it's a good thing he was meeting a woman tonight, if she shows.

He twisted his stool around farther to get a better look at the hottie.

If only she was his date. The woman's blue dress hugged her curvy body, and he couldn't take his gaze off those legs that seemed to go on forever.

Oh no!

One minute she remained all grace, next her poise went down the drain as her shoe broke. Mac lurched to his feet and ran over to help the stunning woman.

"Are you hurt?" He reached his hand out to help but instead of the tears he expected, Mac heard laughter coming from under the waterfall of hair which hid her face. He ached to touch the burnished-bronze length. *She reminds me of Dad's favorite colt, a little skittish, but feisty. I like spirited women.*

Not wanting to see her sitting there on the floor, Mac scooped her up in his arms. *Whoa.* She was like a foal, all legs, and she fit perfectly in his arms. He could hold her all day.

"Sir, is the woman okay?" The bartender stood in front of Mac. He couldn't tell if the guy wanted to grab her out of his arms for himself or to protect his hotel from a lawsuit.

Mac couldn't help but growl like a dog defending his territory. "I haven't checked yet. She appears fine. Why don't you get her a glass of water?" Anything to get rid of him. He wanted to keep her in his arms.

Mac pulled her close to his chest. At the thought of letting her go, his heartbeat sped up. *Maybe I can convince her to have a drink with me.* He reluctantly set her down in a chair at one of the bar tables.

"Are you okay?" Mac brushed the hair back from her face.

The strands felt like silk between his fingers. Images of brushing this woman's hair while they lay naked on the bed danced through his mind. Reluctantly, Mac pulled his hand from her and took a deep breath. He didn't understand what had come over him. He didn't have this strong of a reaction when he met Claire.

Like uncovering a present on Christmas morning, he could hardly wait to see her face. He watched as the woman lifted her head to meet his gaze. Mesmerized by the light dusting of freckles across the woman's nose, his breath stopped. Her beautiful green eyes sparkled with merriment. Her tantalizing laughter danced across his skin making his slacks already tight and very uncomfortable.

"Miss, are you fine? Do you hurt anywhere?"

Trying to bring himself back to reality, Mac ran his hand along her ankle feeling for any broken bones. His gaze traveled up her legs to the tantalizing view of where her dress met her thighs. Who was he kidding? He didn't want to keep his hands off her. She was like a drug. One he wouldn't mind being addicted to.

Once again caught by her softness, he skimmed his fingers over her calf to the bottom of her knee before he realized what he was doing. Mac thought he heard a moan before her laughter stopped.

"Only my pride is broken, I'm sure I made a horrible impression. My date has probably bolted for the door." Her husky voice reminded him of smooth bourbon.

Mac shook his head. Did she say date? What are the chances? While he'd been fantasizing about this little filly, she'd been looking for him. She was his date. How had he not recognized her? He wanted to do a little victory dance but he'd just look stupid. No reason to ruin his chance with her.

"Is your name Lauren? I'm Mac, your date, and as you can plainly see I'm not headed for the door." The blush tinting her cheeks delighted him.

"You're my date?" Laughter bubbled up then escaped with each word she spoke. "Here I tried to be graceful, only to fall flat on my face. I'm not usually so inept. These shoes are truly torture devices." Lauren slipped off her other shoe before holding out her hand. "I hope you aren't too disappointed. Maybe Master Draikoh can arrange for a different woman for you."

* * * *

A fusion of heat mixed with sizzling energy zinged up Lauren's arm as she shook his hand. She had to suppress a delicious shiver at his touch. He had the hand of a working man, calloused and strong. She almost purred at the thought of such hands on her body.

Her gaze roamed Mac's face. His good looks took her breath away. He was even more handsome in person than his photo. His hair looked shorter also scruffy. The cleft in his chin and the chiseled cheekbones confirmed this sexy man standing in front of her was in fact her date. Giddy with her good luck, Lauren couldn't stop from giggling then laughed outright as confusion filled his gaze. She grabbed the unbroken shoe off her other foot before walking over to the bar.

I feel like it's Christmas morning and my present's right in front of me. She longed to fall on her knees and praise God for such a wonderful gift. But one goofy move a night happened to be her limit. No sense scaring him away before she got to know him.

"Thanks for checking on me. No harm, no foul." Lauren spoke to the tall bartender who'd also come to her aid. "Do you have a garbage can around here?" With the nod of his head, she handed him her shoes. "Toss these in there, please."

Lauren looked back over her shoulder, noticing Mac still sat where she left him. She flashed him a smile then all but skipped back toward him. Her brow furrowed as she drew closer and saw his confused expression had remained. *Is my underwear showing or something?* Self-consciously, Lauren smoothed her dress down over her hips then shrugged her shoulders. *I guess I'll find out soon enough.*

"So you're my date. If you still want me," she introduced herself with a smile.

"Of course, I want you. Erm…that didn't come out right." Mac laughed. The sound sent tingles up Lauren's body. "Are you okay? You fell and then threw your shoes away. Most women throw a fit over shoes. I've seen some wail over not getting the pair they wanted."

"I'm not like most women. It's obvious those shoes were plain crap, even though they came with a fancy name and high price tag."

Mac cocked his head while his brow furrowed. He seemed truly perplexed. She couldn't believe he'd never seen a woman throw away shoes.

Baffled or not, Lauren wasn't about to let such a stunning man get away without at least buying her a drink. "Why don't you buy me a drink? We can talk about shoes."

Mac shrugged then smiled. Seeing his smile felt like sunshine after a rainstorm. "Sure, what'll you have?"

"I'd love something fruity. How about a raspberry daiquiri?" Lauren studied Mac as he sauntered over to the deep-mahogany bar. He wore corduroy slacks that hugged his lean legs and tight butt. Oh, she'd noticed him all right. Why does this hunky guy need a dating service? Are those cowboy boots? Since she was a teenager, she'd always had a thing for cowboys. Except for her freefall, this night just kept getting better and better.

While Mac ordered the drinks, Lauren nervously ran her hands through her hair. The two of them were reflecting in the mirror over the bar, but she scrutinized his image. She never had a fling in her life. Except for her ex, she had only slept with one other man. Her stomach filled with butterflies as she continued to observe him. Even as her pulse sped up at the sexiness of the fine-looking man strolling back toward her.

CHAPTER FOUR

Two raspberry daiquiris later, Lauren finally relaxed. She found she enjoyed talking with Mac.

"Are you a cowboy? I noticed the boots." She smiled around the straw in her drink, wiggling her eyebrows.

"I own a few horses," he replied, grinning at her. "I love to ride. I wouldn't call myself a cowboy though. There's something about women and horses. Why do they always interest the women?"

"Hmm, maybe the size of their...." Her face burned. She couldn't believe she said that. "Er...really, it's animals in general. Women love puppies and kittens, too. Give us anything with fur."

"I hear you." His eyes glimmered at her slip of tongue. "Women love fur. I'll let you pet my horse anytime you want." His large smile caused Lauren to snicker.

Their playful banter continued but revolved around animals, television, books, and movies, never getting too personal. Bubbly and charming, that's who she was tonight. She didn't want to bring him down with her worries or let *real life* get in the way of her night to remember. Because she definitely planned on remembering this. She wanted to tuck this night into her heart and bring the memory out whenever she needed a pick-me-up.

Lauren noticed Mac steered the conversation away from touchy subjects as well. Obviously they were both hiding things. That didn't matter though. Their date was for one night, not a lifetime. She wasn't letting her heart get involved.

Mac ran his palm over her arm, causing those goose bumps to flare again. Lauren shifted in her chair as her tingling pussy dampened her panties further. She took a deep breath through her nose, thinking about the things yet to come. She felt like a virgin on her wedding night. As she anticipated pleasing this tantalizing man, the echoes of James's taunting filled her ears. Pushing the negative memories down, she wasn't going to let his harsh words color her date. She wanted to delight Mac more than anything since he engaged her mind and her body.

Ready or not, she was going to make a move. Swallowing the last of her daiquiri in one gulp, Lauren hoped the alcohol would fortify her courage.

"Let's head up to the room. I'd like to spend time with you alone." Lauren's voice came out more breathless than she intended. After Mac tossed some cash on the table for their tab, she grabbed his hand and drew him toward the elevator.

* * * *

They entered the posh elevator. The walls were a gold which reflected their images back at them.

"What a pretty elevator. Look, we're all alone." Lauren's eyes sparkled. Mac watched as she licked her lips then bit on her full bottom one. His heart beat faster.

Mac looked at the reflection of his body standing behind hers. His cock ached. It had been hard since she walked into the bar. He imagined her taste. Would she taste like raspberries or spicy like the bourbon she reminded him of?

Mac leaned around her to push the button for their floor. Bending closer to her shoulder, he inhaled her scent. It was a mix of flowers from her hair and the musk from her desire.

Taking a deep breath, Mac pulled back before looking into her eyes. "I've been wanting to kiss you since I saw you." He pushed the button to halt the elevator.

"What's going on?" Lauren stared at him.

"I can't wait for the room." Mac pulled her into his embrace then nibbled on her neck. He trailed his lips along her jaw toward her mouth before kissing her deeply. *Oh God.* She tasted like sweet white chocolate. Her moan vibrated into his mouth. He ran his hands through her hair. It was as silky as it appeared. He pulled her closer so their bodies were touching from lips to toes. She had no other choice but to feel how much he wanted her. Mac ran his hands down Lauren's body to grip her butt. Pushing his tongue deeper into her mouth, he felt her heart beating against his chest. Leaning toward her ear, Mac whispered, "I can't wait to taste you. Open to me."

Mac slowly pulled aside the neckline of Lauren's dress exposing her breasts. He bent his head down then took her nipple between his teeth and gently tugged. A gasp escaped Lauren's lips. His cock strained against the zipper of his pants. *I didn't think I could get any harder. I love hearing her passion.* He sucked, drawing the nipple into his mouth, eliciting a moan from her lips.

"Your mouth tastes like sweet chocolate yet your skin tastes like peaches. I can't get enough. You're a feast for my senses." Desire made his voice deepen.

Mac pushed Lauren back against the wall then kneeled on the floor. He lifted the hem of her dress. *Damn, her panties are in my way.* Mac yanked on the fabric and was rewarded with a satisfying rip. Lauren gasped again. Her responses were music to his ears.

"Look at me, Lauren," he demanded as he lifted her

destroyed underwear to his nose and inhaled. "Mmmm...I wonder if your pussy will taste like peaches, too." A glazed look of passion entered her eyes as he tucked the panties into his shirt pocket. "Oh, Lauren, I can't wait to savor you."

Her deep uneven breathing echoed around them. She arched her body closer to his mouth. Mac ran his tongue over her swollen lips, lapping at her juices. "Yes, sweet Georgia peaches. My new favorite fruit."

Another moan escaped Lauren, inviting Mac to pleasure her more. He took her clit between his teeth then gently bit down. Lauren's moan turned to a scream. Her orgasm flushed her skin deep pink, eliciting a matching moan from Mac. Sweat broke out on his forehead from holding himself back as he straightened her dress. He scooped her up in his arms when her legs gave out.

"Let's get to the room. I can't wait to feel you wrapped around me." Pushing the button to start the elevator, Mac wished the thing moved quicker.

* * * *

Lauren felt weak as tears welled in her eyes. How had this man rocked her world so completely? She'd only met him a few hours ago. Her thigh brushed against Mac's crotch. She felt his cock pushing against the zipper of his slacks. Poor man. At least she was getting her money's worth in the passion department. More importantly, she wasn't to blame for the lack of satisfaction during her marriage. To think she actually just had sex in an elevator. Giddiness raced through her. Lauren wiped the tears not allowing them to fall. She took a deep breath then lightly kissed Mac on the cheek.

"Thanks for making one of my fantasies come true. Wow." Lauren pasted a smile on her face. She needed to tell Mac just how important their elevator moment meant to her—how he proved her ex wrong.

As the elevator doors opened, Lauren tensed and felt her face warm. Thank goodness no one stood there waiting, she'd have been mortified.

But she realized she had nothing to be ashamed of. She relaxed into Mac, raising her head. He gave her a wonderful gift. She felt empowered, sexy, and desirable. "Let me down, please. I need to walk to the room under my own steam. Trust me, I'm not going anywhere but I need to let you in on a little secret."

"I hope you're not going to tell me you're married or this was all a setup." Mac's face crumbled at her words, his voice held a note of anxiety.

"No. I need to share with you why this date is so important to me." Lauren grabbed Mac's hand and led him down the hall to their room. "After you hear my story, I can *show* you." She winked at him causing a silly grin to break out on his face.

Lauren used the key, opened the door then held her hand out indicating he should enter. The room defied expectations. The décor appeared plush and tasteful yet still held a touch of lived-in feel. The large windows that overlooked Lake Michigan were the focus of the room. The view sparkled with the moonlight on the water. Lauren approached the caramel leather couch, sat down, and patted the seat next to her. She owed it to him to be honest. No matter how difficult it would be to share.

She took a deep breath. *I can do this.* She bit down on her bottom lip, hoping he wouldn't think less of her. "Mac, I'm divorced." Lauren tilted her chin to her chest. She hunched her shoulders as if she needed to hide.

"Yeah, so. Is that your big news?" Mac lifted Lauren's face and gazed into her eyes.

"No. My husband cheated on me with a girl from his office, but even before his affair, he didn't want sex with me. He blamed me, said I was a cold lay and lacked anything a real man would want. His words made me feel like I was somehow inadequate, yet your...our passion in the elevator helped me see things differently." Lauren smiled. "I can't thank you for helping me understand I wasn't the problem."

Mac pulled her closer. "You're a passionate woman, Lauren. I've never wanted to make love to someone as much as I do now." Placing her hand on his crotch, his voice deepened when he spoke. "This is how much I want you."

His cock felt like iron underneath her hand. "Do you have a hammer under here?" Lauren felt it lengthen under her hand. *I can't believe I do this to him.* She gripped Mac's face and placed her lips on his for a kiss. Nibbling gently on his lower lip, she heard him moan. Feeling empowered, Lauren began unbuttoning his dress shirt. "Oh, I love your chest hair. I want to run my fingers through it. Hairy chests are a fantasy of mine. I love being able to indulge my desires with you."

Mac quickly pulled off his dress shirt then threw it off to the side of the hotel living room. "Touch me to your heart's content…as long as I get to return the favor." The mischievous glint returned to his eyes. He slid Lauren's dress off her shoulders down to her waist.

Her breath froze in her lungs. Her nipples puckered when the air hit her naked flesh. *I'm freezing yet on fire from his gaze. Everywhere he looks my skin feels like it's scorched. My breasts are aching for his touch.*

Lauren ran her fingers along Mac's collarbone. She trailed them lower toward the chest hair she longed to touch. The dark curls felt coarse but soft under her fingers. As she gently tugged at them, she noticed his breathing speed up. Lauren bent to kiss Mac's neck. Opening her mouth, she sucked lightly on the tender skin of his neck then nibbled on his skin. Mac's body arched toward hers. The muscles of his chest tantalized her as she traced each before moving her hands in the direction of the waist of his pants. Lauren unzipped his cords and then opened them. She was pleasantly shocked to find him commando.

Sliding her hand up and down the length of him, she watched his cock swell and a drop leak out. Empowered by his reaction, Lauren bent her head. She licked the cum from the tip before taking his shaft into her mouth. Mac's moan echoed in the silent room.

"Oh God, Lauren. If you don't stop, I won't be of any good to you." He pulled her up then kissed her passionately, entwining his tongue with hers. "I can't wait to feel you around me."

Quickly they removed their clothes. Mac pulled a condom out of his wallet before sheathing his shaft. Lauren watched, aching to be the one touching him. *I can't wait to feel him buried deep inside me. His musky smell is driving me wild.* As the condom slid tight over his velvety skin, a shiver ran up her spine.

Mac sat on the edge of the sofa, pulled her body close to his then settled her over his rock-hard cock. A breathless whimper escaped from Lauren's lips. She gripped him tight, but he had gone only part of the way inside. Lauren wiggled arching her breasts. His cock slowly slid home. Finally, he was fully inside her. She sensed her orgasm beginning and yearned to move. "Touch me. You feel so good." Lauren trailed her hands over her breasts. She heard Mac's breathing speed up. He put his hands around Lauren's waist, raised her up, and set her down on his penis. Each thrust drove his rigid cock deeper into her moist folds. Their heavy breathing gave way to moans as their passion exploded.

"Thank you." Lauren nuzzled close into Mac's torso, once again reaching for his hairy chest. Curling up into his arms, she sighed. "I hope you know you're amazing. You were wonderful."

"No, thank *you*. I can't believe anyone thought you were lackluster. Let me run a bath then we can clean up before we do this again. We have all night."

Delight and passion filled the night for Lauren and Mac. They made love in the shower, on the couch again then finally in the bed, falling asleep in each other's arms.

Dawn broke through the windows. "I've got to leave," Lauren whispered to Mac, her shoulders slumping. "You're just the guy to breach the walls I've built. I can't afford another heartbreak. You made me feel so special tonight. I'm sorry." Lauren gathered her clothes then dressed.

"Wait." The shock of her upcoming departure show on his face. "Give me your number. We can work this out." Mac jumped out of bed. "I could see you being the one for me. Draikoh San knows his stuff. I can't lose you. We haven't even had a chance to explore what's going on between us."

He reached out then pulled Lauren into his arms. Tears filled her eyes. "I can't, Mac. I'm scared of what you already mean to me." She drew away and picked up her suitcase before heading for the door. "If we're truly meant to be, something will bring us together again." She quietly closed the door.

Lauren felt her heart break with the click of the door.

CHAPTER FIVE

When Lauren returned to her classroom after spring break, the weight on her shoulders felt much lighter. The time off had refreshed her. Sleeping in helped, too. She'd worked hard to keep Mac off her mind during the day. But the nights were filled with passionate dreams of them making love. Not giving him her number had been the right thing to do. She might have caved in and called. Her dreams of him were steamy, leaving her waking up wet and aching. The physical attraction amazed her, but the connection terrified her. He really could have been the one for her, if she wasn't so afraid of getting hurt again. It didn't matter, right now she needed to focus on her career. At the very least she knew she wouldn't turn into another old cat lady. Lauren ran her fingers over the new nameplate. *Miss Walsh.* At least they got it fixed.

Melanie left voicemails daily, asking about the date, which Lauren avoided. She wasn't ready to share the intimate night with anyone. Let alone Mel who'd see right through her need for the quick exit.

I needed to walk away. Leaving was the right thing to do, Lauren rationalized. She didn't leave because of fear. Besides, a relationship wouldn't work between them—no matter how much passion they had. So why did it sound like she was justifying her actions? Lauren put her face in her hands and took a deep breath, attempting to clear her mind for the upcoming day.

"Why is the first day back always the hardest?" The door opened and shut with a bang. "Thanks, buddy, for calling me back. I'm dying to know how your date went." Melanie flounced into the room and stood toe-to-toe with Lauren.

"The date was nice." Lauren avoided Melanie's gaze.

"Nice? Details, girl. I need to know if he rocked your world."

Lauren's face turned red. "He did. I'm glad I tried the dating service but I really don't want to talk anymore."

Melanie scrutinized at Lauren's face. "All right. I'm glad you had a good time. We can drop the conversation. I also have news." Melanie practically danced around the classroom. "I'm seeing someone but it's hush-hush. I'm not even supposed to tell you." Melanie's face scrunched into a pout. "So don't ask, even though I know you want to. I'll let you know when I can."

Melanie's always about the drama. "Okay, Mel. I'm glad you've found someone. He better be good to you. Or else...dum...dum...dum." Lauren smiled at her with a wink.

"Are you ready for the students to return? I'm sure they're going to be excited to get back to school today." Sarcasm dripped from Melanie's lips.

"They always are. I have everything planned. Did you see the new nameplate? We'll have to remind the students about my name change. I've been thinking a lot about Todd. Worrying, really. He's such a sweet boy but since his mom died, he's had a hard time getting along with the other kids. His loud voice and his frustration lead to throwing or giving up. I want to do more for him."

"We met with his aunt at the beginning of the year. Do you think we should sit down with his family again? I heard his father's home now and taking charge. We can arrange to meet with him this time."

"Let's see how things go now that we're back to school. Maybe the week off made a difference for him, too." Lauren hoped she spoke the truth, but a ball of anxiety settled in her stomach. Her nurturing instincts wouldn't let her stop worrying about Todd.

* * * *

Mac pulled his car into the parking lot of Kingston Elementary. Todd's excitement had him ready to jump out of his seat, whether the car was stopped or not.

"Whoa, buddy. Wait. I'll walk you in."

"No, Dad. I'm good. There's Steven. I'll head in with him. Bye." Todd quickly opened the door and dashed toward the crosswalk and the blond boy waiting to cross. Mac could hear his son call out for the boy. Steven turned and waved at Todd.

Todd enjoying school left him glad. He never really did.

Mac watched to make sure Todd made it into the building. He noticed a figure in the classroom near the school entrance. *Whoa, who's that woman?* The distance from his car to the window made it hard to see her clearly, yet Mac couldn't stop admiring her figure. *That beautiful shape looks so familiar. Where did he know her from?* Perhaps he was just missing Lauren. Everyone he saw reminded him of her. He'd done nothing but think of her every day since she left.

He caught sight of Todd and Steve entering the classroom where the brunette woman stood outlined in the window. *Oh, she's Mac's teacher.* Maybe he'd seen her around town. He would have to go in and introduce himself. His night with Lauren taught him to be more open, not hide as much as he had. Mac glanced at his watch. But he'd have to introduce himself another time. He needed to get to the station. News waits for no one.

Mac put his car in reverse, proceeded out of the school parking lot then headed off to the station where he put the finishing touches on his latest news report about The Playhouse. Maybe he would get lucky. Lauren might see the piece and contact him. He'd tried everything to find her. Even Master Draikoh was silent on the matter. One night together and he was obsessed. Could this be love? Would he even know love if it bit him in the ass?

* * * *

Lauren walked the children out to the curb at dismissal. She blew at the strands of hair that escaped her ponytail again. The first day back after a break took a lot out of her. *I'm sure I look a mess.* "I'm glad everyone had a great break. I liked hearing about your vacations." She watched as a group of students climbed on the first bus then continued to monitor all the students leaving the school.

"Bye. See you tomorrow, Todd," one of the students called out.

"Bye, Steven," he called back.

Eventually all the children boarded the buses or left in their cars. Only Todd remained. When a blue sedan pulled up to the curb, Todd grabbed Lauren in a massive bear hug. She couldn't help hugging his small body back.

"I'm glad you had a good day, Todd. See you tomorrow."

"That's my dad," he shouted. The excitement evident in his voice. He clasped her hand and began to pull her toward the car before it even came to a halt.

"Wait for the car to stop, Todd." Lauren kept Todd safe close by.

The driver's side door opened and out stepped the man from her late-night sexual fantasies, *Mac.* Her mouth dropped open. What? Why is he here? Her mind raced with unanswered questions. Todd pulled his hand out of her grasp before running toward the car.

Mac only had eyes for his son. When Todd launched himself into his arms, he pulled him close then looked up at the woman standing on the curb. As his gaze met hers, Mac's eyes widened.

"Hello, again," he said. His deep voice sent chills down her back. Lauren stood staring at the man she dreamed of each night.

"You're Todd's dad?" Her voice shook. Stunned, Lauren paused in shock.

"Dad, Dad, Dad...." Todd tugged on his dad's arm. "Let's go. I'm ready to go home." Todd's impatience evident to everyone.

"I've been searching for you. I tried to find you. I even contacted Draikoh San. He wouldn't tell me your full name or give me your number." Mac took a step toward Lauren.

She couldn't believe he'd thought of her, too. "You did?" Maybe this was God's way of telling her something. After all, she did say if they were meant to be.... Lauren's thought trailed off as she noticed Todd's desperation.

"Dad...Dad...I want to leave." Todd's body shook. He jumped up and down trying to get his father's attention.

"Just a moment, son." Mac walked over toward Lauren with a purposeful stride.

Is he going to kiss me? Excitement over Mac's body being this close to her took her breath away. She held her breath and closed her eyes. *Please, please.*

She gasped as Mac brushed a stray strand of hair behind her ear. To be this close and not be in his arms. A sigh escaped her lips.

Todd's loud wail echoed in the parking lot and Lauren opened her eyes.

"I've been wanting to see you since you left. Todd's not going to let us talk now. Can I call you later?"

Lauren's face felt warm. She glanced around to see if anyone else noticed their display. Indecision weighed in on her. Should she give him her number? She walked away once because she didn't want to be hurt. Mac could still break her heart. Lauren remembered about how lonely she'd been this week, how she'd dreamt of him, and how she missed his smile. She looked down. Yep, cowboy boots. She'd even missed his cowboy boots. She smiled ready to take a leap. "Sure. Let me give you my number."

Lauren ran back into the classroom and quickly wrote her name and number down on a sticky note. She needed to begin taking chances. She didn't want to be a lonely old spinster regretting letting Mac go. Lauren ignored Melanie's strange look as she rushed back to the curb. Needing answers, she could hardly wait to talk more with Mac. The complications seeing Mac will cause were scary, especially since he's Todd's dad. Another risk. Yet, another chance at happiness.

"Thanks, Lauren, I'll call you tonight." Mac put Todd in his car seat and climbed back into his car. As he drove away, Lauren let out another sigh. She turned to see Melanie staring at her.

"Wow, Lauren. What was that all about? I could see the smoke between you two from inside the classroom. He's a hottie and all, but should you give your number out to a stranger?"

"Melanie—*he* was my perfect date from The Playhouse *and* Todd's father. I didn't know who he was when we had our night. What a mess." Frustration colored Lauren's voice. Her face felt on fire. "I walked away from him, never expecting to see him again."

"Karma really loves you, Lauren," Melanie answered with sarcasm then noticed the horror-filled look on Lauren's face. She reached out and gave Lauren a hug. "I'm sorry. The situation sounds tough. At least, you didn't fall in love."

With those words, Lauren's heart skipped a beat.

CHAPTER SIX

Todd's chatter about school filled the drive home as Mac thought back to his night with Lauren. At last he found her. He was determined not to let her get away this time. Returning to what Todd was saying, Mac paid closer attention as his son's excitement showed how much he adored Lauren. She'd connected with him in a unique way that allowed Todd to enjoy school even after his mother's death. He knew she was special. What other woman showed such passion in the bedroom as well as a dedication toward forming positive relationships with children. Lauren could never be like Claire. Maybe he fell for her the moment she threw those shoes away. Each thing he learned about her—each facet—made him want to know more.

Todd continued to prattle on about his friends, the games played at recess, and his favorite part, lunch, but Mac couldn't keep his mind on his son's words. Lauren filled his thoughts. Seeing her standing there on the curb shocked him. He'd spent the last week constantly mulling over what he'd done to scare her off, and how to find her. Wishing he'd had time to prove they were right for each other. Maybe this haphazard meeting will provide a second chance.

Mac thought about Lauren while making dinner. His need to see her again was overwhelming. He read a story to Todd that luckily put him right to sleep. Mac wondered if she thought about him. He wanted answers and planned on getting them. He vowed it.

* * * *

Melanie convinced Lauren they needed to talk. Her friend must've felt the need to rail on her decision to give out her number. Dating a parent is a major no-no, no matter how strongly one feels about the person. It wasn't fair she made such a connection with Mac only to face ridicule from her friend.

She and Melanie headed out for a drink after work. Lauren still felt like a deer in a pair of headlights. She couldn't believe Todd's dad was the man who went down on her in an elevator. *Oh the things we did that night.* A blush settled on her face.

"I have to explain about the date. I tried to put the whole night from my mind, yet I couldn't. I kept thinking of him."

"I wondered why you didn't want to share that much. But I didn't want to pry."

"Mel, the encounter had everything, not only desire, but we formed a real bond. We talked and laughed. You know I wouldn't have gone through with it had I known he happened to be Todd's dad. It's too late. I can't take back my feelings either." Lauren grimaced after taking a large swallow of her drink. The alcohol burned her throat.

"I know you wouldn't fall for a beautiful face. You haven't dated since your ex dumped you. Could your feelings be because you were caught up in the emotion of the sex?"

"I suppose. Although I doubt it. His interest in my thoughts and our talks about life in general demonstrated to me we'd joined on more than a sexual level." Despair choked Lauren, causing her voice to crack. "The depth of my feelings scared me, that's why I gathered my clothes and ran without finishing the weekend. I had hoped never to be tempted by him again. Now, how do I deal with him as someone I have strong emotions about as well as a parent of one of our students?"

"Look, maybe this is a sign. You guys were meant to be, but you need to know all the facts—he *is* a parent. That's sure to complicate things. I wouldn't want this relationship to cost you your job, too. What would I do without you everyday?" Melanie laughed at her own joke.

Lauren tugged Melanie close then hugged her. "Thanks for the drink and being a great friend. I have to go. He's going to call me tonight. Would you believe he's been trying to find me? He even called Draikoh San. Hopefully we can talk things out and make a decision about where we stand."

"Just be careful. I don't want you hurt. Now, shoo. I'm meeting someone in a bit." Melanie wiggled her eyebrows. "Remember, no one's supposed to know."

"Sounds like I should be worrying about you and your mysterious boyfriend. After all, if you can't be seen together, he must have something to hide. I don't want *you* getting hurt."

Melanie gave Lauren a shooing motion. "I'll see you at work. Go so your prince charming can call." A big smile filled Melanie's face.

Lauren left the bar. A man walking in the back entrance caught her gaze. *Is that Principal Stevens? What's he doing here?* Lauren dismissed the thought then headed home. She couldn't get Mac out of her mind. Why did he have to come back into her life? Him being a parent will muddy the water even more. Her mind raced. "What am I going to do?"

Lauren turned her car onto State Street when her phone rang. Could that be Mac? She felt her stomach do a little flip as she answered.

"Hello. Is this Lauren?"

Lauren bit her lip to keep calm. "Yes, it's me. Hi, Mac. How are you? Thanks for calling. I'm sorry for my shock today." Lauren pulled her car into the local grocery store parking lot. She didn't want to take a chance talking while trying to drive. Her emotions were all over the place. Giddy like a schoolgirl talking to her first boyfriend on the phone as well as nervous she'd say or do something stupid. She took a deep breath to calm her speeding heart.

"My feelings shocked me, too. I hoped to see you again after you left. I searched for you. I don't understand why you left. Sometimes I feel as if I dreamt the whole night." Mac chuckled at his attempt at a joke.

"I *needed* to leave. I enjoyed our night so much. Our tryst had to be only one date though. I worried I wouldn't be able to walk away if you offered me more." Lauren sighed before sharing her biggest fear. "You're a powerful man, Mac. You have the power to break my heart. After my divorce, I didn't think I had a heart to break but you showed me differently. Our night restored my passion. I felt more than just desire with you. I couldn't risk you pushing me away, so I walked away first."

"Lauren, I'd really like to talk to you more—face to face. Can you come over? I can't leave Todd here alone. He's in bed. I promise I won't try anything. There's so much we need to say. Over the phone isn't how I want to discuss things." Mac gave Lauren directions to his home. "Please."

The pleading in his voice struck a chord with Lauren. Fluttering butterflies filled her abdomen. The thought of seeing Mac, of touching him, of kissing him…Lauren's breath sped up. "All right. I'll be over." *I hope I don't regret this.*

* * * *

A long driveway led to the white Colonial home. Tall windows stood sentinel on both sides of the ornate red front door. Lauren observed the home as she pulled her car toward the house. The front porch light glowed in the darkness. Marshalling her courage, she stepped out of the car and approached the door. Lauren took a deep breath then knocked. The door swung open showing Mac standing barefoot in blue jeans with a heather-gray button-down oxford shirt. A smile broke on his face when he looked at her.

Seeing the smile on Mac's face caused her stomach to clench. Immediately, she remembered the way his lips felt on her neck. Shivers tumbled down her spine.

Misinterpreting her shivers, Mac spoke. "You're cold. Come in." Mac held the door open then indicated the way to the kitchen with a wave of his arm.

"Your home is beautiful. I've always loved the older homes. They have more character. The darker oak flooring gives your home a warmth. Although this looks like you've modernized the kitchen. I love to cook. A modern kitchen is a must. Do you enjoy cooking?" Worried she was rambling, Lauren sat at the kitchen table.

"I make a mean Sunday breakfast, but that's about it. Can I get you something to drink? Water? Soda? Lemonade?"

"No, thanks. Now that we have the small talk out of the way, did you know I taught Todd?" Lauren scrutinized Mac's face for any sign of lying. She'd become adept at noticing lies after dealing with her ex-husband.

"I never knew. School and Todd weren't really even Claire's area. My sister did all of Todd's carpooling while I worked overseas. Up until Claire's death, I served as a foreign correspondent reporting on the unrest around the globe. My home became wherever the latest conflict occurred. I know this sounds horrible for Todd's sake, but Claire and I weren't *comfortable* around each other." Mac blushed as he took a seat. "Explaining this to you is the hardest thing I've done. I don't want you to think less of me. Things were out of my control." He ran his hands over his face.

"I'm glad you're sharing now. I want us to be honest with each other." Lauren empathized with his pain. Her own marriage crossed her mind. Claire seemed to be a lot like James. Image had meant everything to them.

Mac raised his head and looked into Lauren's eyes. "To be honest, she only desired my money. She wanted a rich husband. I fit the bill. What I wanted didn't matter to her. But I only wanted to escape her high society desires. In fact, she made Todd's and my life hell when I tried to fight her. I didn't want to lose my son. I felt I made the choice I did to protect him. He's really close with my folks spending a lot of time with them." He took a deep breath staring at the tabletop. "I didn't tell you those things about me during our night on purpose. I was more interested in you, just *you*. You're so different than Claire. Your shoe incident melted my heart. To you, money didn't matter."

Lauren's laughter filled the kitchen. "Those shoes nearly killed me. You're right. Shoes nor money are important in the scheme of life. I'd rather be happy." Lauren pushed her hair back off her face and into a ponytail. "I must look a mess."

"Thank you for being so accepting." Mac reached up and ran his hand along her hairline before caressing her cheek. "You are so beautiful." He pulled her in close, bending his head and kissing her deeply.

"Mac." His name became an entreaty from her lips. She pulled back, putting distance between them. "We can't. I deserve more than being a booty call. I want more." Lauren raised her chin. A relationship, not just sex or friends with benefits. These were non-negotiable. But how can she tell if Mac was serious?

"I know all the reasons why we shouldn't, but I can't help myself. I feel a connection with you. You're a funny, compassionate and desirable woman." Mac focused on

Lauren, holding her gaze. "I want to explore our relationship." Lauren opened her mouth as if she might say something. But Mac raised a finger to have her pause.

With the nod of her head, Mac continued. "Before you deny it, we *do* have a relationship. I know you feel the same. I want to date you. I need to show you how good we are together. Honestly, I can't let this go…let *you* go, without trying to see what might happen. Let's turn our perfect date into something more. Come with Todd and me this weekend. We're visiting my family's stables. With Todd along, you won't have to worry. I'll behave."

"Yes." With only one word, Mac lit up like a Christmas tree. Lauren ached to drag him off to bed and forget about all the drama. Just love him.

He pulled her into his embrace then kissed her. As his tongue passed along her bottom lip, Lauren felt her heart beat faster. Mac ran his hands over her butt and pulled her tightly against his body. "Feel how much I want you," Mac snarled before deepening their kiss.

She pushed back against Mac's body, loving the feel of his strength against her. She sighed. Being with him would be so easy to do. His touch burned her. She melted when he was near. But she couldn't forget her divorce or Mac's position as a parent. *I wish I knew the right answer.*

"Lauren, I want nothing more than to lay you across the table with the way you're creating those sexy little moans, but I'm going to be a gentleman. I want to win your heart, not just your body." Mac took a deep breath then stepped back. Emotions played across his face, tightening her heart. "I'll pick you up Saturday morning at nine. Dress for riding."

Mac led her to the door and stole one last quick kiss.

Lauren couldn't stop tapping along with the music as she drove home. She was so excited she couldn't stop moving. She wanted to shout to the heavens about Mac's feelings for her as well as her feelings for him. She needed someone to talk this through with. *Melanie.* Picking up her phone, she hit speed dial.

A groggy voice answered. "Hel...lo...do you know what time it is? You know I'm going to kill you, right?"

"Mel, sorry about the time. I couldn't think of anyone else to talk to. I have a date." Lauren could hear the excitement in her voice.

"A date? I know this is a *freaking* miracle, right up there with a flying pig, but why wake me up?"

"It's Mac. We're going to see what's going on between us. I'm nervous in addition to excited. I haven't felt this way ever. We're going to his family's farm." She beat a staccato rhythm out on the floor of her car.

"Oh, I've thought about this, Lauren. I know a friend's supposed to be supportive but I've had time to mull things over. Do you think seeing him is wise? I don't want to be a party pooper but he's Todd's dad. *A student's dad.*" Her voice held conviction. "I know I egged you to sign up for this date. I also know Draikoh's success rate is high. However, he must have made a mistake in this case. You can't date a parent at school. People will talk. You'll get *fired.* Obviously, Draikoh San didn't have all the information."

With those words, Lauren stilled. Could he have really made a mistake? No one's perfect. Her shoulders slumped. Fired? They wouldn't fire her. She was allowed to date who she wanted, right? There was nothing in the employee handbook about dating rules. Lauren furrowed her brow as she thought it over.

Lauren heard a male voice in the background. "Who's on the phone?" The voice sounded familiar. Where had she heard it? The phone distorted the sound so she couldn't tell. She knew it was someone she knew though. Lauren's eyes opened wide as she realized what she interrupted. Mel still had her mysterious boyfriend over. She'd spoiled their night.

Finally she spoke, sadness filled her voice. "I'm sorry to bother you. I forgot you had company. We'll talk at school.

Night." Lauren quickly disconnected then pulled her car off the road.

Melanie sure had a way of bringing her down. She also changed her tune pretty quick. Just earlier today she listened then urged her to go after him, and now it's like Mac's got the cooties. Mac may be a parent, but he's the one she was falling for. The question was which could she risk losing out on—a job or love? Lauren returned her car to the road. Her drive home became a somber one.

* * * *

Yawning, Lauren could hardly open her eyes. Even with the sunlight pouring in her window, her head felt full of cotton. She didn't get any sleep last night. All that tossing and turning. Thanks to Melanie, her panties were in a twist. She finally found a guy she liked, a guy she could—is falling for, and her best friend goes and tells her it's not meant to be. Why did she listen to her fairy tale to begin with? Lauren picked up her pillow and threw it at her door.

Glancing at the clock, she jumped out of bed. "Crap." No time for a shower today, she'd just throw her hair back into a ponytail again. She brushed her teeth then quickly picked out the first outfit she glanced at before looking at the clock again.

"No time to make breakfast or pack a lunch. I'll have to take my chances at the cafeteria." She grabbed her purse, keys, and computer before heading out to the garage. Lauren sped all the way to the school. Melanie was always early. Surely she'd gotten the morning message up. Instead of worrying about her tardiness, Lauren tried to focus on the day's lessons. She wasn't watching and ran smack into Principal Stevens who was leaving her classroom.

"Oops. I'm sorry." Lauren felt her face warm. *Great.* On the day she's late, she runs into the principal. This was bound to set a good impression.

A smile blossomed on his face. "No problem. I'll let you get into your classroom." The smile showed off a couple of dimples she'd never seen before. He was sort of handsome if you liked the suit and tie type. He certainly should smile more.

"Hey, Mel, sorry I'm late. Did Principal Stevens need something? I saw him leaving. Is there a problem?"

Melanie ducked her head. "No, nothing important. Just stopping by to check on the room, see how our class is doing."

"Are you okay? You look flushed. Your voice sounds strange, too. I'm sorry for calling last night and interrupting. I heard a voice, so your mysterious boyfriend must have been over. I thought I recognized him but I couldn't place his voice. Still can't tell me, huh?" Lauren noticed Melanie couldn't meet her eyes. *Hmm.* Mel's usually the first to share about her sexual adventures. She's never silent about her guys. Maybe it's serious. "All right never mind, I'll just forget I might know him. I needed to talk—to explore why my feelings are so strong. Just don't tell anyone about Mac's and my relationship, okay?"

"I won't. Although it's sure to get out. We live in a small town. You're seeing a big reporter. Someone will say something." Melanie bent her head when she spoke, hiding her eyes. "They'll think you are giving Todd special treatment because of his dad. The school's reputation will suffer. You've heard about those teachers doing bad things in the news. I don't want your story to end up there."

"I'll be careful. Besides you know I won't treat Todd differently. We better get ready for another busy day." Putting an end to the conversation, Lauren went over to the board to write the day's schedule for the students.

Now to survive the week. Lauren felt like she could dance each time she thought of the weekend. However, her mood soured when she saw Todd walk through the classroom door. *What will Todd think of me coming over?*

CHAPTER SEVEN

Saturday morning finally arrived. Lauren hadn't slept well the night before. Excitement over seeing Mac again overwhelmed her mind. She'd scoured her closet trying to find just the right outfit. Mac had said dress for riding. *That'll mean jeans.* Luckily, she had some old cowboy boots. Lauren pulled her hair into a ponytail before adding a little makeup. She looked in the mirror. This was as ready as she'd ever be. Hopefully Mac would like the way she looked. She smiled as she thought about seeing Mac again. She placed her hand on her stomach. *These butterflies better stop.*

The doorbell rang. Lauren thought her heart might jump out of her throat. She walked slowly to the door. Don't want to appear too excited, she rationalized as she opened the door. Todd and Mac stood on her porch. A smile lit up Mac's face. The grin showed off a small dimple in his chin. Lauren couldn't resist smiling back. Her stomach felt like there were squirrels not butterflies in there.

"Hi, Mrs. Fulton. Is this where you live? I like your boots. They're way cool. Dad says we are going riding today. I haven't been to the stables in a long time.

Grandma and Grandpa live there. Do you like horses? Have you ever ridden one?" When Todd didn't look like he would stop for a breath, Lauren noticed Mac's smile change to a scowl. She smiled at Todd then broke into his diatribe.

"Yes, Todd. Remember to call me, Miss Walsh. My name changed."

"Oh, yea. I forgot. Sorry, Miss Walsh." Lauren nodded at Todd. She cracked a grin at his contrite face.

"It's okay, Todd. I'll keep reminding you. Now the rest of your questions…I like horses and used to ride when I was younger. I had a wonderful stable near my house. I'd go with my friends. We'd ride almost every day. I wanted to be a trainer but I decided to be a teacher instead."

"Hi, Lauren. We'd better get going. It's a bit of a drive yet."

Looking back at Mac, she was caught off guard by his looks once again. He wore dark denim jeans that molded to fit tight against his thighs and ass. *I could stand here, watching him walk in front of me all day.* She wondered how his assets would look on a horse. As Mac turned to walk back toward his car, a sigh escaped Lauren's lips.

He glanced over his shoulder. "Did you say something?"

"No. Just let me grab my purse and cell phone. Thank you for inviting me." After grabbing them quickly, she locked the door. *What have I gotten myself into.*

Todd continued to provide the conversation as well as entertainment for the drive. He had something to say about everything including sharing random facts about the different breeds of horses and sizes. Mac's silence soothed Lauren's nerves. She noticed he'd chew on his thumb cuticle every once in a while. Maybe he was nervous, too. At least Todd served as a distraction for her own anxiety. She smiled as she gazed at Todd again. He's such a great kid. She didn't know why she was worried he'd be upset about her coming along.

After a two-hour drive, the car slowed down in front of a tall. black iron ornamental gate. It looked like those gates from the big Texas Hollywood TV shows. The house or barn were nowhere in sight. It was obvious Mac came from a prestigious family, but she couldn't imagine growing up around all this wealth. Fortunately, Mac had turned out well rounded, not pretentious at all.

"Are we here?" Todd sat up straighter, looking around.

"Yes. My family's farm has been home for the Thomas family for decades. My parents live here now. I can't wait for them to meet you. We'll drive over to the barn so we can ride. After the ride, Mom planned a lunch."

The anxiety in Lauren's stomach grew. She put her hand to her churning stomach. They're not squirrels anymore but gazelles leaping and running. Holding back her fears wasn't an option, she had to say something.

"Mac, you didn't mention your parents were going to be here. Isn't this a little soon for the meet-the-parents event? I'm not even sure they're going to like me. I don't hang with the country club crowd. I'm a coupon cutter who loves shopping at discount stores. I have money to live comfortably but I'm not extravagant. I'm just a small-town teacher."

Mac placed a hand on her cheek. "My parents are going to love you. First of all, you don't have to be anything you aren't for them. Dad's still the one who cleans the barn each day and cares for the horses. Not because he has to but because they're a passion of his. Mom will want to know all about your secret discounts. She still saves and reuses her plastic baggies. They aren't the ostentatious wealthy people you think they are."

Lauren let out a deep breath. "Thank you for explaining about your family. It's important for them to like me if we are to have any relationship. I'm scared." She grabbed Mac's hand and gave it a squeeze.

Mac returned the gesture, smiling at her and flashing his dimples once again. "Besides, they'll like you because I do."

Lauren couldn't stop staring at Mac's dimples. *Those little dents are going to be the way he gets whatever he wants. I can see how things will be now.*

Mac put a quick kiss on Lauren's cheek before punching a number into the keypad by the gate.

"Ewwww." Todd's face scrunched up showing his disapproval. "Kissing's gross."

The large gate swung open. As the car headed down the drive. Lauren lifted her chin. *New Lauren, remember.*

* * * *

Lauren could tell Todd felt right at home in the saddle. He had a way with the animals from the big gelding to the tiny, newborn barn cat. He not only loved animals but looked like he enjoyed caring for them. This was a side of Todd she could use. Maybe he could help with the fish in the library or share his love of animals with the students. The other children deserved to see this side of Todd, rather than the one who's always frustrated.

Lauren let her gaze roam over Todd. He's such a sweet kid. Getting to know a different side of him by spending the day together has been great.

She enjoyed the tranquility of the ride. Her horse, Comanche, walked slowly making her feel very comfortable. Besides, she had the best view of Mac's backside. He did look great in the saddle.

"Lauren, you're a natural rider," Mac said sounding amazed as he pulled his horse up next to hers.

"I used to ride each week at the local stables but when I left for college, the stable closed. I haven't ridden in years. I guess it's like bike riding, you never forget." Smiling, Lauren ran her hand along her horse's neck. Mac picked the perfect horse for her. His gentle walk and spirit helped her relax. The sunny weather yet cool temps made the ride even more enjoyable. Beautiful scenery filled their ride. Todd loved pointing out the different animals he saw.

"Todd, you're so good with the animals. Do you think you'd like to help take care of the fish in the library? I know Mr. Stevens could use some help."

"Wow. Could I? I'd love to." Todd's smile filled his face, reminding her of Mac's. She noticed the similarities, now she could see them next to each other.

"I also thought maybe you can do a report for the class on horses. A lot of the girls love horses but don't know as much as you do. Maybe teach us all something. Would you like to share your knowledge with the class?"

Todd's smile grew bigger. "Dad, will you help me with the report?"

When Todd looked toward his father, Lauren could see his smile fade. That's interesting. Worry and hope filled Todd's pleading eyes.

"Of course, buddy. I'd love to help. No worries. Maybe we can get Grandpa to take some photos of his horses so you can put them into the report."

Lauren continued to watch Todd's expression. She noticed the change immediately when Mac agreed. Todd appeared to need the validation of his father's support and attention. She filed the information away for another time. There's a lot she was learning today about the puzzle that is Todd. She climbed off her horse, gave him a nuzzle on his neck, and helped the guys put the horses into the barn.

Mac walked over and put his arm around Lauren as they watched Todd playing with the kittens again. "You're really good with Todd. What did you see I didn't?"

"Todd waits for your approval before he commits to something. He wants you to accept him. I'm sure a part of it's because of your wife's death. Loss profoundly impacts a child. I've been so worried about Todd because of his frustration. He lashes out in school."

"I know what you mean. I've seen similar things at home. I wish life had been different for him, but I just couldn't live up to Claire's needs. My son became the one to suffer."

"The good news is kids are resilient. Todd's a wonderful young man. I think with your interest in him and school, he'll be okay. Although, you may want to consider counseling. It'll help to have someone else for him to talk with and maybe help with the frustration. Can you imagine being upset but not knowing how to put your feelings into words? That's what's going on with Todd."

"He's lucky to have a wonderful teacher like you." Mac embraced Lauren, holding her body tightly against his.

Lauren could feel his breath on her cheek and smelled the odors of the barn. "I'll never forget this moment."

"Nor should you." A strange male voice piped in.

Heat filled Lauren's face. *Oh, no. Who's this?* She pulled away from Mac's arms.

"Sorry. I didn't mean to interrupt. I'm Mac's dad, John. I agree with Mac. Todd's lucky to have you. You're right about my grandson."

Lauren focused her gaze at her feet, unable to meet John's eyes. *I can't believe he caught us snuggling in the barn. What a great first impression. What will he think of me now?*

Mac pulled Lauren toward John. "Dad, your timing stinks. But since you're here…this is Lauren Walsh. Lauren, this is my dad."

John stuck his hand out. Lauren's eyes were still downcast. "Now this won't do." He gently raised Lauren's chin looking her straight in the eyes. "Nothing to be ashamed of. I'm glad to meet you. We speak our mind here. We hold no tolerance for fakes."

"Grandpa." Todd screamed, running toward John. Todd's distraction gave Lauren a chance to observe the older man. His white hair looked distinguished. John stood a little shorter than Mac but they shared the same build. *His dad does look like a cowboy, not a Forbes billionaire. It's nice to know what Mac's going to look like in twenty years or so.* John's face lit up as he listened to Todd ramble on about the ride, the kittens, school, and everything else

Todd could think of.

Mac took a hold of her hand. It was nice to have someone to lean on. She could get used to relying on Mac, his strength, his passion.

"Your dad seems nice," Lauren whispered in Mac's ear. "I can't believe he walked in on us."

"Like I said, he's going to love you," Mac whispered back as he kissed her neck. Lauren laughed before playfully shoving Mac away.

John flipped a squealing Todd over his shoulder and faced Mac and Lauren. "Come on. Mom's got lunch on the table."

* * * *

The petite ash-blonde-haired woman met them in the kitchen. Her welcoming smile warmed the room. "Come in. Welcome, Lauren." She walked toward Lauren before motioning to the kitchen island. "I've got cold cuts for us. Everyone can make their own sandwiches. I wasn't sure what everyone would want. Todd, I have your favorite, ham. Make sure you eat. You're a growing boy."

"If he gets any bigger, I won't be able to do this, anymore," John said breathlessly as he set Todd on his feet. Once standing, Todd ran to hug his grandma.

Lauren took this chance to look around the kitchen. The room appeared bright with sunny yellow walls and knickknacks of farm life decorating the space. A large wood trestle table dominated most of the area. It's old marred tabletop held a warm, lived-in feel. This wasn't what she'd expect from billionaires. She'd have thought the house would have chrome and sleek lines, not a country down-home feel.

She watched Todd's grandparents, running her previous beliefs against reality. They didn't look like billionaires either. Mac's mom wore faded jeans with patches on the knees. Her no-fuss hairstyle reminded

Lauren of how many times she pulled her hair back instead of dealing with it. John appeared to have stepped out of the television screen of old shows like Bonanza or The Big Valley with his leather vest and worn cowboy boots. Instantly Lauren relaxed. Her shoulders dropped as she smiled. They obviously adored Todd, doting on him.

Maybe this won't be so bad. James's criticisms created such anxiety in her. She never felt good enough, but there—among this family—she felt like she belonged.

"There are kittens in the barn, G'ma. Did you see them? Can I take them some ham? Did you meet Ms. Walsh? She's my teacher. She said I can take care of the fish at school."

Laughing aloud, Todd's grandma pulled him close before giving him a squeeze. "Todd, we'll talk about all those things. First go wash up then we'll eat."

Todd ran down the hall into another part of the house.

Mac tugged Lauren's hand, dragging her over to his mom. "Mom, this is the woman I'm going to marry."

Lauren's body froze as her mouth dropped open like a largemouth bass, gasping for air. Recovering quickly, she pasted a smile on her face. "Mac, you didn't just say marriage. Quit teasing your mom. Hello, Mrs. Thomas." She gave him a playful shove before reaching her hand out to shake his mom's.

"It's nice to meet you. Call me, Joann. I'm sorry, Lauren. Those Thomas men know when they've found their mates. John wouldn't take no for an answer when we were dating. He proposed fifteen times."

"She turned me down only fourteen though." John walked over and kissed the top of Joann's head. Laugh lines around their mouths and eyes showed their age, but also showed how much they enjoyed living. Their gazes held a deep warmth of love. That long-lasting love is what she wanted in a marriage. A person to laugh with and who loves deeply.

"How long have you two been married? It's obvious

you're still so much in love."

"We've been married going on forty years. Never a dull moment." Joann's voice sounded with happiness as she looked at John.

"I'm sure there isn't. However, Mac and I just met. We're not getting married," Lauren stammered.

"Yet!" Mac's voice boomed across the kitchen.

Everyone but Lauren laughed at Mac's joke. Lauren's mind reeled. *Does Mac really feel so strongly about me? More importantly how do I feel?*

CHAPTER EIGHT

After the lunch with his parents, Mac and his son became a steady fixture in Lauren's life. Idyllic weeks passed. Mac and Lauren avoided the scrutiny of the school by spending most of their time together at their homes or the ranch. Lauren believed by not thinking about the conflict, the controversy would just go away.

She hardly spoke to Melanie out of fear she'd hear about her relationship again. Some people would say she's avoiding things. Maybe, yet she was the happiest she'd ever been. She had more energy for the daily outbursts at school, feeling calmer and more patient. Other people even noticed. Her relationship with Mac was the reason. There was good coming from their being together. Even Todd had shown a huge improvement. He gave his presentation about horses the other day. When the whole class applauded she felt so proud. Seeing his face light up with the recognition brought tears to her eyes.

Though Lauren's days were wonderful, her nights were astonishing. They spent each evening together, sometimes making dinner as well as helping Todd. Other nights, they went out dancing with his parents or watched the stars from the hayloft. *It's working. I've fallen for him.* They hadn't spoken about forever, nor made any declarations of love. In fact, they hadn't made love since that first night. Mac had been so chivalrous. He told her he wanted to win her heart before her body. He appeared to be setting out to romance her, showing he's the man for her.

Sitting on the couch in Mac's living room, Lauren sighed. Mac pulled her closer into his arms.

"This has been nice spending time with you. I've enjoyed getting to know you." Lauren winked at Mac. "Yet, I'm missing something."

"Tell me. I'll make everything better. Nothing is too good for my future wife." Mac's voice held a note of laughter. Lauren reached over to swat Mac on the head.

"Stop with the wife thing. You've been so romantic but we've done nothing more than share a chaste kiss these last few weeks. I miss your body." Lauren heard her voice deepen with her want.

"Let's give you what you need. I'm glad my folks have Todd for the night." Mac pulled Lauren onto his lap. He kissed her deeply before gently biting down on her bottom lip. A moan escaped Lauren's lips when she felt Mac's cock harden underneath her. She wiggled closer to ease the ache between her thighs, increasing the kiss. She darted her tongue into Mac's mouth, teasing his. Without breaking their kiss, Mac unbuttoned her blouse and slipped it off her shoulders. Next came Lauren's bra straps. Mac bent his head and took her nipple into his mouth. He sucked on it then nibbled gently, running the taut peak through his teeth. Moaning again, she threw her head back, allowing Mac better access to her breasts. A warmth crept across her skin as Mac toyed with her nipples, lavishing care on one then the other.

"I can't wait to feel you inside me." *Is that my voice? I hardly recognize it.* Lauren stood, removing her clothes. Standing before Mac naked, she ran her hands over her body. "I love watching your face when you look at me with desire. I feel so beautiful, more than I ever felt before."

Mac reached for her, but she backed away. "Not yet."

He growled, standing and stripping off his own clothes.

She stared mesmerized as Mac's body came into view. The dark hair dusting his chest dipped lower down his firm abdomen toward his jutting cock. Lauren forgot she was supposed to be teasing him when Mac put his hand on his penis, rubbing the length up and down.

Mac growled again. "I'm done playing. Get over here."

Lauren liked the bossy side of him.

"Where's a condom?"

He bent down then pulled one out of his wallet.

Lauren grabbed the wrapper and ripped it open with her teeth. She rolled the condom over his rigid shaft. Moistness coated her folds as her stomach clenched in anticipation.

"Come here and bend over." Mac moved next to the couch.

Eager to comply, Lauren placed her knees on the cushion of the couch then bent over the back of it. She arched her back before looking over her shoulder at Mac. Lauren licked her lips as she squirmed with eagerness. "Please, Mac. I want you. Fill me."

"You feel so good. I can't wait." Placing his hands on her hips, he abruptly pushed his full cock into her pussy. Mac began to thrust, quicker and more forceful with each plunge.

"Oh, God. Mac, yes." Her voice rose with each drive.

Mac had taken charge, forcefully thrusting his shaft into her body, groans escaping his mouth. Pulling Lauren close, he bit down on her shoulder as their orgasms rocketed through their bodies.

Spent, Mac lay his head on her shoulder.

Lauren moaned. "Now that's what I needed. We need to make love more often."

"Anything for you." Turning her around, Mac kissed her nose before taking her into his arms and carrying her to his room. "Let me get rid of this condom." She looked around as he disappeared into the bathroom. But didn't have time to see much as he returned and took her in his arms.

"Please stay the night, Lauren. Todd won't be back until lunch tomorrow." Mac's voice held a note of urgency. "I long to hold you and watch you sleep."

"Mac...I'd love to stay the night." Lauren reached up, ran her fingers through his hair then kissed him passionately.

"We have all night together." Mac gently laid her on his bed.

"I can't guarantee we'll get much sleep." She wiggled her eyebrows at him.

Reluctantly, Lauren headed home the next morning sated and tranquil. She'd been right. There hadn't been much sleeping going on.

* * * *

Mac's decision to romance Lauren left her very little time for her friendship with Melanie. She missed having her friend around to bounce ideas off of, and to be silly with, or talk to about men. So, she made plans for drinks after work.

They drove across the street to their favorite Mexican restaurant. After selecting a high-top table in the bar, the girls flagged down a waitress and ordered drinks and chips before beginning the gabfest.

"You've been seeing a lot of Mac. How are things going?"

"We are spending almost every day together. Last weekend we went on a picnic to the zoo with my family. They adored him. Mostly we do family type things, cooking dinner or hanging out at his parent's house." Lauren felt giddy with excitement. "Mac told his parents we would marry on our first date to their farm. Isn't that cute?"

Melanie snorted and margarita shot out of her nose.

"Oh, Mel. I'm sorry. I should've warned you." Patting Melanie on the back, Lauren signaled the waitress for more napkins.

Coughing and sputtering, Melanie looked like a drowned rat, but at least the flood of margarita from her nose had stopped. "I'm fine. What do you mean *wife*? Has he proposed to you? Are you engaged?" Lauren thought Melanie's eyes might pop out of their sockets.

"Girl, I need deets," she sputtered out.

Lauren wiped up the mess on the table as she composed her thoughts.

"Are you sure you're okay? You look like a frog. Positively green. Calm down. He didn't propose. His mom told me Mac's dad acted the same way. Supposedly Mac's dad proposed fifteen times before she agreed. I guess the Thomas men are single-minded when they decide they've met the one."

"Have you met the one?" Melanie whispered. "You know James railed on how you looked, acted, well…everything. I don't want you to leap with your eyes shut."

"I'm not." Conviction filled Lauren's tone. "Mac's the one for me. I've never been able to be myself more than when I'm with him. The sex…." A blush heated her cheeks. "It's amazing. James thought I had the problem. I don't with Mac." Lauren leaned into Melanie's ear. "We even had sex on the kitchen table."

Melanie covered her mouth. Lauren pulled back and nodded. Her friend's eyes grew gigantic once again.

"Okay, so sex isn't the problem. What about Todd? Have you considered his reaction? How does he feel about you two dating?"

"I haven't spoken with Todd. Mac wants talk to him, just the two of them. However, Mac and I make sure Todd feels included. We date as a family most of the time. He's always happy. You've seen how much he's improved at school."

"I have but Todd's still your student. Mac—a parent. We can't make the issue go away." Melanie stared hard at Lauren.

"Mel, Mac wants Todd to be in our class. He's seen how much we've helped him. Besides our school allows children to be students in their parent's classroom. Todd's situation is no different. I love Mac. I don't know how or when my feelings changed. They just did. If he asked me to marry him, I would. Then anything about Todd being my student would be moot."

"It's not the same, *now*." Melanie shook her head.

"Why would it be a big deal if we do get married? I know we haven't dated very long. But Mac's been perfect. We have so much in common. Besides, I'm allowed to remarry." Lauren saw skepticism cross Melanie's face.

"Still, Mac's a parent of one of your students. We've gone over this before. People will talk…. In fact, I've heard rumors about your relationship. You know the gossip mill at work. Someone's going to push the issue. You'll be fired."

"They can't say who I date. What I do in my time off work is my own." Anger tinged her voice. "Who's talking?"

"I've just heard things. No one in particular. But Todd *is* our student. You aren't his parent, *yet*. That's a conflict of interest."

"What? Don't tell me you believe I'm handling him differently? You can't think I'm giving Todd special treatment. I can't believe you'd side with them." Tears pooled in Lauren's eyes. Grabbing her purse, she pulled out money to leave for the waitress. "I thought you were my friend. Friends support each other."

"I *am* your friend. I'm trying to help you. You need to know what's being said. Your job and reputation is on the line." Melanie reached out to grab Lauren's hand, but she pulled away.

Lauren stormed out of the restaurant. tears streaming down her face.

* * * *

While Lauren met with Melanie, Mac had planned his own guy time—going to the movies with his son. They'd returned to the house for dessert.

"Wow. That's quite an ice cream sundae, Todd. Are there really twelve cherries on top? Hey, you forgot the whipped cream. Would you like some?" Mac held the can out toward Todd.

"Oh yea. Thanks." Todd accidentally sprayed whipped cream on the counter and all over Mac's shirt. "Ooops. I'm sorry, Dad."

"No biggie. Let's wipe this up then I'll go change." This kind of accident used to annoy him. But then Todd's accidents had always set his temper off. "I think this is the first accident you've had in a long time. You must be growing up." Mac smiled at his son. So much has changed since Lauren came into their lives. Mac grabbed the dishrag and washed the counter. "You finish your ice cream. I'm going to change shirts."

Mac walked into his room and opened his bureau drawer. There he noticed the old blue photo album. Forgetting about changing his shirt, he pulled out the album and started to rifle through the photos. A sigh escaped his lips. How many kids believed their parents are crazy? He did. Looking at them, one could certainly see they enjoyed being together and the love in their faces. Dad pretending to be a horse with Sherry on his back was always a photo opportunity. Mom holding her and laughing. He remembered the next picture well. Mom was in the pool with him watching Dad doing a cannon ball. He loved drenching everyone. Mac was focused entirely on the photos, so he never heard Todd walk in.

"Hey, Dad, what'cha looking at?"

"These are pictures of when my parents, your grandma and grandpa, were younger. Some of the photos are of me and your Aunt Sherry as kids. I've been thinking again about the story they told the a couple of weeks ago at lunch about their wedding."

"Yea, they tell *that* story all the time. How come they keep repeating it?"

"Because it's important to them. The story reminds them of what they went through to get married. See, here's their old wedding ring." Mac held up a simple white gold band with a marquis cut diamond.

"Ooohhh. It's sparkly. Can I see the pictures?"

Mac handed the album to Todd before studying his son sitting next to him. He had come out of his shell in the past month. The outbursts all but disappeared, and Todd's confidence had grown along with his friendships. "Todd, what do you think of Miss Walsh as your teacher?"

Todd turned toward Mac, with his face scrunched up. "She's a nice teacher. She treats everyone nice. She never yells. She's even shared her lunch with some of us when we forgot a snack or something. I still don't get subtraction and borrowing but I'm trying. Why, Dad?"

"I just wondered. Do you like spending time with her at home?"

"Yea. You seem so happy. You kiss a lot." Todd made a face then stuck his tongue out. "As long as she doesn't try to kiss me, I'm good. Although one of the kids didn't believe she used to ride horses. He said I fibbed about her coming to Grandpa's barn. He called me a liar. But I'm not."

"No you aren't." Hesitant to bring up the subject, Mac needed to know. "What if she wasn't your teacher anymore?"

A puzzled look crossed Todd's face. "I guess she can't be my teacher when I'm in high school. It's in a different school. I like her. I'd miss her if she wasn't my teacher."

"What if you got to see more of her? Like riding, visits to the zoo, and stuff? If she wasn't your teacher, would it be better?"

"I guess. I'd get to see her more. Do you think she'd be sad if she wasn't my teacher?"

He grabbed his son and held him tight. Mac spoke softly. "I know she would. Let's get ready for bed." Mac grabbed the album then put the memories away. He pocketed the ring though. *I've got Todd's blessing. Now I have to find a way to convince Lauren. Hopefully she won't make me ask her more than once.*

* * * *

Lauren didn't want to go home to an empty house, so she drove to Mac's house, replaying Melanie's harsh words. How could her best friend take their side? She wanted Mel's support. She felt betrayed by someone she trusted, which hurt almost as much as what James did. Tears fell down Lauren's face. Lauren glanced in the visor mirror. Her face looked puffy and red from her tears.

She knocked quietly on Mac's door, preferring not to wake Todd. When the door opened, Lauren launched herself into Mac's arms.

"Whoa. What's going on? Honey, are you okay?" Mac pulled her close to his chest. "Let's go inside. You can tell me what's going on."

"I'm sorry to bother you. I couldn't go home. I needed to see you." On the sofa, Lauren curled into Mac's arms as she told him all about her conversation with Melanie. She wiped at the tear stains on her cheeks. Just being with Mac made her happier. Together they were a team.

"I love the way you fight for us. I love you. Can you forgive me for making such a mess of things? I'm sorry our relationship causes you stress. I never wanted these problems to happen. You've been the best thing for Todd. *For me.*" Mac bent in and kissed her.

Mac's kisses clouded her mind. Did she really hear those words? She knew he meant them. Lauren felt her heart rate jump.

"Oh, Mac. I love you, too. I'm willing to fight for you because you've made me into a stronger woman." She returned his kiss with vigor.

"We'll make our relationship work. I promise." Mac gazed into her eyes.

"I know we can. Thanks for being here tonight. I needed your understanding. I've got an early morning tomorrow. I plan on talking with Melanie before the students arrive. She's always been a friend. I don't like fighting with her. I've got to try to make things right between us." Lauren stood, and Mac followed, tucking a few of her stray hairs behind her ears.

"I love you," he whispered. "Drive safe. I'll talk to you soon."

"Me, too. Night," Lauren responded as she headed out to her car. The day filled her thoughts on her drive home. In bed, her dreams left her body yearning and craving Mac.

CHAPTER NINE

Lauren's alarm sounded like a buzzer to her sleep-deprived brain. She'd tossed and turned all night wishing for Mac's hot body. She slammed her hand on the alarm to stop the awful noise. Remembering last night, Lauren felt like dancing. *Mac told me he loved me.*

Then she remembered her fight with Melanie. She had to make things right. Lauren hopped in the shower then got ready for work. She felt determined to get her friendship back. She knew just the thing, she'd stop by the bagel shop, pick her up a bagel and her favorite flavored coffee. At least then they can talk before the students get there. She was sure Melanie didn't mean to hurt her feelings. She grabbed her bags and left the house. Her step light, almost prancing.

When Lauren arrived in the classroom, she saw Melanie and Mr. Stevens were waiting along with a person she didn't recognize. She glanced at Melanie, trying to catch her eye. But Mel wouldn't meet her gaze. Something's up. If this was about last night's fight, Principal Stevens wouldn't be here.

"Hi, Mr. Stevens, Hello, Mel…I'm sorry I don't know your name. Did I miss a memo about a meeting?" Lauren put the coffee and bagel on Melanie's desk. "I brought these for you. I'd hoped we could talk." She turned to the other people in the room. "Had I known you all were going to be here, I'd have brought more." She shrugged her shoulders sheepishly.

"Hello, Ms. Walsh. We need to talk." *Oh no. He's acting all serious. What did I do?* Lauren thought back through the last few days. Nothing came to mind.

"My students will be here in about fifteen minutes. Can we do this after work?"

"I'm afraid not. I've arranged for Mrs. Johnson here to sub in your room until we can finish our meeting." Mr. Stevens's voice remained calm yet authoritative. His tone brokered no-nonsense. *I don't think I'm going to like this.*

Lauren raised her chin but she put a smile on her face trying to be pleasant. "All right. Let me get Mrs. Johnson settled. I need to give her the lessons for today. How about I meet you in your office in ten minutes?"

"I'll see you there." With Mr. Stevens's departure, the tension fled the room. Melanie ran over to Lauren.

"I didn't have anything to do with this. I tried to tell you." Her face showed a mess of concern.

"What's going on, Mel? What are you talking about?" Lauren stood toe-to-toe with her best friend, her arms crossed in front of her.

"Mr. Stevens knows about you and Mac."

"How'd he find out?" Again, Mel couldn't meet her gaze.

"Well...do you remember when I told you I had been seeing someone? The man I'm dating is Keith Stevens...Principal Stevens." Melanie's voice broke on the final word.

"What? You're seeing our boss? You told him. That's how he knows about my relationship." Anger crawled up from inside. She wanted to scream, imagining throwing the bagel at her head. Lauren took a deep breath before she spoke. "I thought you were my friend. I know we had a fight but I thought we'd work things out. I even brought the coffee and bagel as a peace offering."

"I didn't tell him, but I know a parent reported your relationship to him—which parent, I don't know. I didn't lie to him when he asked me though. I defended you. I told him you weren't playing favorites." Melanie met Lauren's gaze. "I'm still your friend. I tried to warn you."

"So all the time you were hollering at me over who I dated, you were sleeping with the boss? Now that takes balls." She couldn't believe someone would call the principal about this. Who she dates was her own business. At least she knew what she was going before the firing squad about. She considered slamming the door on her way out but decided it wasn't worth it.

Entering Mr. Stevens's office felt like being called on the carpet by your parents. Lauren fidgeted with her bracelet on her wrist. *I won't cry…I won't scream…I can be professional.* The mantra repeated over and over in her head.

"Please have a seat. You've been a teacher here for six years. We've always valued your skills and feel you're an asset to our school. Frankly, your students and their families love you. However, it's come to my attention you're dating a parent of one of your students." Keith plucked a file from his desk and glanced at the page. "A Mr. Mac Thomas. His son is Todd Stone. Is this true?"

"Yes, it's true. However, I'm not treating anyone any differently. I team teach with Melanie, as you know. She's the one in charge of Todd's grades. I don't play favorites or treat any child better than another." Meeting Keith's gaze, Lauren wanted to make sure Keith understood her feelings.

"Well, who you're dating does matter to at least one family. They came to my office the other day, complaining about your relationship." Keith's tone took on a serious note.

Lauren tried to keep the anger out of her voice. Taking a deep breath, she began. "Look, Keith. You, yourself, are dating a teacher, someone you have to *grade*. Do you give Melanie any more promotions or better pay than the rest of us? Our school allows parents to have their own children as students in their classrooms. How are they different than what I'm doing? Besides, this is a free country. No one can tell me who I can and can't date."

"You're right on both accounts but I can't jeopardize the school. I don't want your reputation to suffer. I can't help but sympathize with you, but before this goes to the board or someone requests we fire you, I want to try to fix things." Compassion filled Keith's expression.

"I understand, but you're asking me to choose between love and a student who needs me." Tears filled Lauren's eyes.

"I'm asking you to help Todd as a friend and caring adult…whatever happens between you and Mr. Thomas. I won't ask you to give up your relationship. Ultimately, this decision has to come from you. I'm going to give you the day off since we already have Mrs. Johnson in subbing. This way you can talk things over with Mr. Thomas. But you must let me know your decision tomorrow. At that point, if you haven't decided, I will make the choice."

"So basically you're telling me to allow you to move Todd or you will move Todd. You're not giving me much of a choice." As tears began to fall down Lauren's cheeks, she used her hand and brushed them away. Keith handed her a tissue.

"I know this isn't much of a choice. But if you love Mr. Thomas and want to keep your job here, it's the only choice you have." Keith's expression appeared grim. "I'll see you in the morning with your decision."

Lauren stood in a daze. *Am I dreaming?* Lauren pinched her arm. *Ouch. Not a dream.* She couldn't believe a parent would complain. It's obvious someone had way too much time on their hands or had an axe to grind against her.

She walked back to her classroom to get her purse. As she entered the room, the students saw her and ran to hug her.

"Ms. Walsh, where have you been? We missed you. Are you leaving? What's going on?" The questions flew from the students' lips.

Wiping tears from her eyes, Lauren stood among the students. These kids were her reason for teaching. She loved these kids. She couldn't lose her job. But she couldn't lose Mac. Glancing over at Todd, who stood off to the side, tears filled Lauren's eyes again.

"I've got to go to a meeting. I'll be back tomorrow. Be nice to Mrs. Johnson. I want a good report."

Lauren grabbed her purse and without a word to Melanie or Mrs. Johnson, left the classroom. *There's only one person I want to see…Mac.*

* * * *

Mac's phone rang. He dragged his cell out of his pants' pocket to see Lauren's number displayed. She never called during the day. She should be teaching. Mac's stomach clamped with worry. "Hi, Lauren. Aren't you at work? What's going on?"

"Mac, they found out about us and gave me an ultimatum. Either I break up with you or they move Todd out of my room. I need to see you, Mac."

Mac could hear hiccups from Lauren as well as the tears in her voice. "Where are you? Can you come to the station?"

"They've given me until tomorrow to decide."

The phone got eerily silent. Mac's heart stopped. Fear gripped his stomach. He couldn't live without this woman. He might have been teasing when they first started dating about her being his wife, but at the risk of losing her, she was his everything. The photo album, Mom's ring, along with his talk with Todd cinched things. He and Todd already had the proposal all planned out. He only hoped she said yes.

"Lauren, honey, are you still there? We'll work things out. Remember, I said I'd make this work...make us work. Come to the station. I'll meet you outside."

"All right. I'll be there in fifteen minutes."

When Lauren arrived at the studio, Mac had paced thirty-two times back and forth in front of the building. It felt as if his feet had memorized each step. His mind wasn't on the warmth of the sunny afternoon or the smell of the cars from the nearby overpass. He was fraught with fear over losing Lauren...or worse, hurting his son. There had to be some way to make this right. He'd been in tighter situations overseas. He just had to find the answer.

Lauren's car pulled into the empty space near the front of the station. She climbed out then practically ran toward his open embrace. When Mac kissed her forehead, he saw her red eyes and damp face and his heart turned over again.

He held her close, murmuring, "It's okay. We'll figure out how to make things work."

Lauren buried her face in Mac's chest. "Come on. Let's sit down." He escorted her into his office then closed the door. "Now tell me what happened."

"Keith Stevens, the principal, called me into the office. He's been dating Melanie. Can you believe she's seeing him? She said she didn't tell him about us, a parent went to Keith, but how can she date him? She never told me. Even though she railed on me for dating you."

"I suppose you can't help loving who you love." Mac smiled slightly at the thought. He brushed the stray hair off her face. "So Mr. Stevens gave you an ultimatum?"

"Yes, he said I couldn't date you and still be Todd's teacher. I have until tomorrow to decide, drop you or he moves Todd."

"I know you love Todd, but how do you feel about me? After all, I'm causing all these problems for you. Say the word. It'll be the hardest thing I've ever done but I'll walk away." Keeping his emotions in check, Mac gazed at

Lauren, trying to read her. "Is having Todd in your class more important than what we have?"

Tears flowed freely down Lauren's face. "How can you ask that? I...I...Mac, I can't bear the thought of losing you. I thought it crushed me when my ex-husband dumped me, but losing you would kill me. I love you." Mac held Lauren's face. Gently he kissed her on the lips. The kiss deepened as Lauren put her hands around his shoulders.

Pulling back, Mac looked into Lauren's face. "I love you, too, Lauren. I didn't know I would fall for you so hard. You've made my life better from the first moment I held you in my arms."

Mac pulled Lauren into his embrace once again then kissed her passionately. Mac felt her fingers in his hair as a sigh escaped her lips. She placed her forehead on his.

"We need to fix this problem at work. They can't fire you. I suppose if Todd must be moved, then that's our answer, as long as you're in our lives."

"Mac, those are the words I've longed to hear. Draikoh knew what he was doing when he matched us. Even the problems at work seem smaller when we're together."

"You said a parent complained to the principal, this Keith Stevens, who is sleeping with a teacher, your friend, Melanie?" Lauren nodded. "I don't understand why he's focused on us. Maybe we can use his relationship with Melanie to open some eyes to what's important."

"What do you mean?" Her brow creased.

"Like I said before, you can't help who you love. Should we be punished for our love? Should Mr. Stevens for his?" Mac became more animated as he walked around the office, speaking to himself, seeming to have forgotten Lauren sat there.

Suddenly, Mac stood tall. He faced Lauren. "I need to talk to my director. Will you please wait? I'll be right back." He gave her a kiss before heading out of the room.

Mac walked into the station director's office then

closed the door. A dark-haired man sat in front of a computer. He looked up when Mac walked in. "Hey, Jason. I don't know if this is a story, but I wanted to run my idea by you. Today my girlfriend—my future wife...."

"You know that's not a story, unless you're a Hollywood star." Jason laughed. "Seriously? Congrats. Who'd you get to agree to marry you? I hope this doesn't mean you're going to go back to the big network and do overseas stories. We'd miss you around here."

"No, Jason. I'm marrying Todd's teacher. Here's the story. She was told a parent complained so Todd can't be in her class because of our relationship. All this came from the principal who's dating another teacher." Mac paced the room while explaining the situation. "Can they force her to make that choice? Dictate who can teach whom?"

"I suppose they can. It'd look like favoritism but I'm sure there are incidents where it's happened. We live in a small town. Everyone knows or is related to everyone. I remember the time one of my teachers was an old babysitter. How could having her teach me been totally fair?" Jason stood and paced alongside of Mac. Both men walked the floor, striding and thinking.

Jason stopped then looked at Mac. "I think you should go to the school board about the situation. It's obvious you feel strongly. I have their schedule on my computer." Jason's fingers flew over the keyboard. He grabbed the paper that printed. "Yep. Tonight's the next board meeting. At seven. You can share your thoughts in addition to the facts you find. I don't think they're doing anything wrong, but the decision feels in the gray. Sound good?"

"Sure. I'm going to take Lauren home then we'll be back later for the meeting. I hope they're open to hearing the truth." Mac shook Jason's hand. "Thanks. See you later."

"See you. Best of luck, Mac."

Mac went back to his desk. He explained his decision

to Lauren as they headed back to Mac's house to work on his speech. This was going to be his most difficult on-air commentary. *Probably because it's so close to my heart.*

CHAPTER TEN

Mac and Lauren worked on his speech as a team. They spent the afternoon with their heads bent over the papers lining the table. Together they'd made their decision. Mac's tale tonight at the board meeting would seal their fate.

"Hopefully this will get people talking. Do you need more coffee?" Lauren stood to get herself another cup.

"No thanks. I need to call a few people to finish up things before the meeting. Can you pick up Todd from school? We can tell him together about us...as well as what's going on when you bring him home."

"Sure. It'll give me a chance to see Melanie. We never talked."

"That'll be good. I'd hate to see your friendship slip away. I don't want to come between the two of you." Mac turned, grinning at Lauren.

Lauren couldn't return his smile. Her fears consumed her mind. "I'm worried, Mac. I hope Todd accepts these changes. I'm afraid he's going to hate me. Having to switch classes will be another loss. He's been getting over his abandonment issues, I don't want to bring them back." As guilt ate at her, Lauren looked down at her feet.

Mac walked over to her. "Look at me," he demanded.

"I talked to Todd yesterday. He told me he would love to have you in our lives more, even if it meant he couldn't see you at school. He's a smart boy. He knows he's getting the better end of the deal." Mac grinned as he reached over for her hand then pulled it toward his mouth before kissing each finger. "I know I'm getting the best part of the deal."

Turning her around, Mac patted Lauren on her butt as he pushed her toward the door. "Go get Todd. Talk to Melanie. I've got strategies to finagle."

"I'll pay you back for that later."

"I'm planning on it."

As Lauren closed the front door behind her, she saw a wicked smirk cross Mac's face and wondered what he was up to.

The mellow music on the radio during the peaceful ride to school was lost on Lauren as she thought about her choices and tonight. Without Mac as a distraction, her stomach clenched as nerves started to take over. Tomorrow, things would be different. Tomorrow, Todd wouldn't be her student anymore. And then there was her talk with Melanie. Even though they had fought before, this felt different. She wanted to fix this. *No matter what, she's my friend.*

Lauren parked her car then walked into the school building and entered her classroom. Students ran around cleaning and getting ready to go home. At the sight of her, the noise level grew.

"Let's quiet down." Melanie turned and noticed Lauren, a smile crossed her face. "Hello, Miss Walsh. We're just getting ready to pack up. Can you help?"

Laruen couldn't help the tears that entered her eyes. She loved her job and these students. "Sure. If we hurry, I'll read from our teacher-read book. Can you clean up quickly, quietly, and safely?" The class moved like a wave as they followed the directions.

Lauren walked to the carpet and sat in the teacher chair.

Mrs. Johnson gave her a big smile as she came over to her.

"The students were a treat. Thank you for letting me help out today. They missed you though and spoke about you all the time. It's obvious you're loved here."

"Thank you. They're special kids. I think of them as my own." Lauren looked about her classroom. Her gaze lit on the different children. Each one had her heart. Each one could be a challenge but they were so worth any trial. Her gaze settled on Todd. He wore a big grin surrounded by his friends. What a difference a few weeks makes.

Mrs. Johnson went back to helping the students when Melanie approached her.

"Thank you for the bagel and coffee." Melanie's face showed signs of strain as she stood there. "I'm sorry I didn't tell you about dating Keith. We didn't want it to get around. Our relationship is exactly like yours. Even though I was trying to protect you, my hypocritical attitude must have really hurt you. I'm so sorry I didn't realize. I want to make things up to you, if you'll let me." Her shoulders slumped as her eyes filled with tears.

"I'm willing to give things a try, Mel. You did hurt me badly. While I can't forget what happened, I want to work on forgiving. I'm sure you felt caught in the middle between your best friend and your boyfriend. My feelings aren't as nice toward Keith though. Todd won't be in our class as of tomorrow." She pressed her lips into a tight line while taking a deep breath. She couldn't cry now. This move would be for the best. Besides she'd still see Todd all the time.

Lauren stood and Melanie wrapped her arms around her.

"You can tell me next time I'm being a witch. Just kick me in the butt or something." A glimpse of Melanie's smile returned to her face.

"Oh, I will. I'm here to pick up Todd. Mac's in the middle of something. He can't come. Todd doesn't know yet about the changes." She glanced over at Todd again to see him gathering his backpack and lunch box. She was so proud of him. He'd really made an effort to control his fears. Maybe he should be her example. No more letting fear rule her life.

Students filed to the carpet with their backpacks ready to go home. Just as she promised, Lauren read to them from their teacher-read book. As she matched her voice to the characters', her enthralled audience almost didn't hear the announcement for the buses.

"That's our dismissal. Everyone line up," Melanie instructed.

Lauren walked over to Todd. "Hi, Todd. Your dad asked me to pick you up. Work got away from him. Are you ready to leave?"

"Hi, Miss Walsh. Sure. I'm ready." Todd turned toward Steven. "Miss Walsh is taking me to my dad's house. See you tomorrow." He waved goodbye to Mrs. Johnson then put his hand in Lauren's.

A warmth settled over her heart. This must be what it feels like to be a parent.

"Bye, class. See you all in the morning." Lauren felt her smile light up her entire face. For such a horrible beginning, the day hasn't been all bad.

The ride home with Todd lifted Lauren's spirits more. She enjoyed hearing his perspective on the substitute and the events of the day.

"And then what did Steve do?"

"He said excuse me really loud before he ran to the bathroom. Everyone laughed. Even Steve did."

Lauren pulled into Mac's driveway and smiled. "At least he used his manners."

Lauren glanced at Todd. His smile reminded her of Mac's. She was so lucky to have this time with Todd. It's amazing how much has changed since the beginning of the year.

Mac's parents were sitting in the kitchen when Lauren

and Todd arrived home. Todd ran and jumped into his grandpa's arms. His voice and laughter filled the kitchen. Lauren welcomed the restful feeling of coming home to happiness as well as smiling faces. "Hi, John, and Joann. It's nice to see you." She walked over to give each of them a hug. They'd grown close since she started dating Mac and felt like family.

"I asked them to come tonight for support." Mac grabbed his son, giving him a tight squeeze. "Glad you're home. Go show Grandpa the new book you've been reading. Maybe you can read a bit to him before dinner. I'm sure he'd love to hear you read." Mac winked at his father before Todd dragged John down the hall.

Lauren went willingly into his arms as he pulled her close then kissed her lips softly.

"How did things go with Melanie?" When his gaze met hers, he looked smug like he knew things would work out.

"We talked and settled our issues. I haven't totally forgiven her. Her apology and recognition went a long way though." Lauren shrugged before she turned in the direction of Joann. "I'm glad you're here for moral support. Mac's speech is brilliant. I also appreciate you being here for me. I tear up each time I think about Todd moving to another classroom."

"I understand." Joann grasped Lauren's hand and patted it. She had a twinkle in her eye that left Lauren confused. Was she happy about the move? "Things have a way of working out. I'm glad you'll still be a part of Todd's life, even if you aren't his teacher."

"Thanks, Joann. I'm so very lucky to be in Todd's and Mac's lives. They're two pretty special guys. You did a wonderful job raising them." She smiled at Joann then turned to Mac. Her heart sped up at the sight of him. Will it always jump when she looked at him? "Mac, do you want me to help with dinner? What are you making?"

"We're having burgers. I'd love some help with a salad." He kneaded his stomach. "We don't want to be too full. Nor do I want a nervous stomach with the speech tonight. Come here and help." Mac opened his arms wide.

She walked into them and felt home.

They headed off to the school after dinner, wanting good seats, especially with so many of them attending. Lauren had never been to a board meeting before, so she worried about how it would go. Mac assured them through dinner things were going just like he planned. She thought she'd noticed glances as well as a few winks between Mac and his parents but she might've been mistaken. Her stomach rumbled so she massaged it. Dinner wouldn't settle because of her nerves. She bit down on her bottom lip to calm herself as they arrived at the school. The parking lot's spaces were almost full. Was there another activity going on tonight she didn't know about? Maybe a volleyball game?

Mac grasped her hand. "Quit worrying. It'll all be fine. You'll see. Trust me." His fingers teased Lauren's palm before he kissed her hand. A chill climbed her spine as her legs felt like jelly. Mac resumed the walk into the building.

The board meeting was held in Laruen's classroom. As they approached the door, a great deal of noise could be heard from inside the room. "Oh, Mac, I wonder if they've moved the meeting. The noise is more than a few board members could make."

When Mac opened the door, Lauren's jaw dropped. The meeting was standing room only. Lauren saw the board seated at the front of the room at a table. Very few spots weren't taken by people she knew. Principal Stevens was there, which Lauren expected. However, she noticed Melanie was sitting next to him. Many of the faces were parents of former students, other teachers, as well as staff members, even some of the bus drivers. There were community people, Lauren's neighbors, even Mac's boss from the station. She doubted all these people usually came to board meetings. They must have heard about Mac's speech. Thank goodness she wasn't the one talking, she'd be a wreck. Lauren rubbed her stomach again. The pain in her abdomen had gotten worse. Near some empty chairs, Mac's sister, Sherry, and her family sat.

They approached Mac's sister. "Hi, Sherry. It's nice of you to come to support Mac. He doesn't even look nervous. I'm sure it's because of his job—always used to giving speeches and interviews to important people." Lauren enveloped Sherry in a hug before taking a seat and glancing over at Melanie. She caught her gaze. Melanie gave her a two-thumbs-up salute. Lauren returned her gesture with a smile and a wave. She looked around the room at all the familiar faces, unbelieving so many people cared enough to turn out.

Mac had Todd and his parents settled before taking his seat next to her. He squeezed her hand and patted his pocket before fiddling with his notes.

"Are you ready?" Lauren whispered, leaning into Mac's ear.

"You bet. I've stared down insurgents in Bogota, this will be a piece of cake." Mac kissed her cheek just as the gavel sounded.

"Ladies and gentlemen, due to the overwhelming attendance tonight as well as the special request for an open forum on a school matter, we have postponed our old business and will begin with new business. We're opening the floor to speakers."

As if on cue, Mr. Stevens rose and walked to the front of the room.

Lauren's stomach somersaulted. This is it. She closed her eyes then took a calming breath.

"Hello, board members and esteemed guests. I'm Keith Stevens, the principal here at Kingston Elementary. I'm speaking today on a matter that has come to my attention. A parent came into my office worried about a student receiving preferential treatment. This parent found out the teacher and another student's father were dating. She felt the teacher gave special managing to the boy. I spoke at length with this parent about the situation, only to find out later her child wasn't even in the same classroom."

Chuckles filled the room.

Mr. Stevens cleared his throat before continuing. "A full investigation originated. The teacher in question is the most caring and compassionate teacher we have. She's been awarded Teacher of the Year by our local school board for her drive to go above and beyond with meeting the needs of each student. In her six years at our school, she's made a difference in so many lives. I did recommend we remove the student from her classroom, but only because of my concerns for the school, not because she did anything wrong. I want my opinion on the record. I find her to be an exemplary teacher and an asset to this school."

Lauren felt her face warm with all the praise. She smiled at Mr. Stevens.

"Thank you, Mr. Stevens. We'll take your words under advisement."

He cleared his throat before beginning again. "I'm sorry. There's more. I also stepped over a line. I fell for a teacher on my staff. We dated secretly so no one would find out or complain. However, I want to come clean. I love Melanie Whitman."

Lauren quickly looked over at Melanie. Mel's hand was covering her mouth. Lauren saw tears in Mel's eyes when she stood and approached Keith in front of the room.

Mel reached out to take Keith's hand. "I love you, too." She then regarded the audience. "I'm ashamed to say my behavior almost cost me the best teaching partner and friend I have. Lauren Walsh put up with my nagging about her choice even while I hid my own relationship. Thankfully she's given me a chance to redeem myself." Mel blew her a kiss. "If anyone thinks Miss Walsh would change how she treats a child because of who she's dating, they don't really know her. Those students are all her children. Each one is treated like the unique and loving child they are." Melanie hugged Keith. They both returned to their seats as applause filled the classroom.

"Thank you as well, Miss Whitman. You've given us a lot to think about."

Since Lauren's eyes were on Melanie and Keith, she missed seeing Todd rise and head to the front of the room. When she turned around, her breath hitched in her chest. What's he doing up there?

"Hello. I'm Todd Stone. My dad is dating my teacher, Miss Walsh. I've always felt special to Miss Walsh, even when she wasn't dating my dad. She treated me like I could do anything. She wanted to know what I liked. She always works with me even when I'm frustrated. I used to be really angry and worried after my mom died." Todd's voice squeaked. He cleared his throat.

He looked so grown up. He couldn't have done this just a few weeks ago. Lauren's heart exploded with love.

"Miss Walsh never got mad at my behavior. Nothing changed when she and my dad dated, except we went horseback riding and to the zoo. She has the coolest boots. Did you know she rode horses when she was younger? Anyway, she's the best teacher. You can ask Steven or anyone in my class. Nothing's changed her teaching."

As Todd ran back to them, she stood and hugged him tightly. "What a beautiful speech. I can see you have a lot of your dad in you." She couldn't believe this young man so eloquently defended her.

"I'm so very proud of you, son." Mac pulled him into his own hug.

Todd beamed. His smile brightened his face. He kissed his dad then climbed onto his grandpa's lap.

"Looks like it's my turn." Mac kissed her cheek before walking to the front of the room.

The room silenced. Mac stood up straighter then patted his front pants' pocket.

"I'm Mac Thomas. The reason we're here tonight has to do with me. I fell in love with the most caring, compassionate woman in the world. I didn't know who she was when we met and began dating." Mac paused, glancing at Lauren.

He's going to make me cry. So much for trying to hold it together.

"On our first date, she literally fell into my arms then threw away a pair of two hundred dollar designer shoes. Her smile and laugh attracted me. Subsequently, she walked out of my life. Devastated doesn't begin to explain how I felt."

Tears began to flow freely down Lauren's cheeks. Sherry handed her a tissue then stroked her arm.

"Fate blessed us when I ran into her here. I hadn't known she was Todd's teacher nor did she know about me either. Karma, fate, God. Something brought us back together. We spent more time together, got to know each other, and fell deeply in love. Love doesn't always decide where your heart is going to go. Mr. Stevens loves a co-worker, someone he *grades*. Should he be punished? Should he lose his job or have Melanie transferred to another school?" Mac paused, as murmurs filled the classroom.

Lauren wiped at the tears flowing down her face. She couldn't be more proud of Mac. He'd spoken from his heart.

"Yet, Miss Walsh, who has been described as an exemplary teacher had to make the choice to give up love or her job which fills her with passion. She's the best teacher this school has. She's made a big difference in so many children's lives including my own son's. I don't want her choice about love to cause her or Todd to be picked on or targeted. I want everyone to know the decision to move my son was made under duress. We weren't really given a choice since some parent got a bee in their bonnet about our relationship. A parent who doesn't even have a child in Miss Walsh's class." Mac took a breath. His voice remained loud yet strong and carried toward the back of the classroom as he continued.

"Today teachers like Lauren are hard to find and even

harder to keep. They work long hours, attend conferences to improve their skills. They create lasting relationships with their students and families. Kingston needs to recognize them and not worry about appearances. What's more important—an excellent teacher or reputation? I know what's important to me."

Mac walked over to Lauren. He held his hand out to her, but she shook her head. "I can't," she whispered.

"Please. Stand with me. Show them you're the amazing person I know you are." Mac's begging moved Lauren.

She stood and put her hand into Mac's. They walked back to the front of the room. Butterflies filled Lauren's stomach. She'd always been more comfortable around the children than adults. But with Mac by her side, she could do anything.

"I never thought I'd find someone who made me feel the way you do, Lauren. I'll never ask you to be anything than who you are. Nor do I want you to give up your passion or your love of your students." Tears continued to flow down Lauren's face. Mac reached up to wipe them away before he put his hand in his pocket. When he bent down on one knee, Lauren stopped breathing. *What's he doing?* She noticed the classroom became silent.

"Lauren, I've found the perfect love with you. You accept me, make my life exciting, fill my soul with joy, and make me a better man." Mac opened his hand and held out his mother's wedding ring. "This ring belonged to my parents. They gave it to me with their blessing. I want us to have the loving marriage they do. Will you marry me?"

Lauren didn't need to think about her answer. Mac gave her the strength to be herself, never belittled her quirks, and showed her true love really existed. The entire audience appeared to be holding its breath as they waited for Lauren's response.

"Yes. I'll marry you."

Mac placed the ring on Lauren's finger. *Am I dreaming? I can't believe I'm going to marry this wonderful man. It's all because of Draikoh San and The Playhouse. Another successful match.*

Applause broke out. Whistles and catcalls were heard. The classroom erupted into chaos. Todd covered his ears to shut out the din. Mac pulled Lauren into his arms then kissed her deeply. The hoots became louder. Melanie, Mac's sister, and his mom ran up to congratulate them.

A gavel sounded on the table. "Call to order," the board president called out. The classroom became quiet again. "We see this situation requires some thought and discussion on our part. Thank you to everyone who spoke today. It's obvious Miss Walsh is a beloved as well as dedicated teacher. We wish more teachers were like her. Bylaws need to be adapted to encompass situations like this one in addition to Principal Steven's situation. We'll have a report at our next board meeting. In the meantime, congratulations Miss Walsh and Mr. Stone. We wish you all the best. This meeting is adjourned."

Lauren felt the strength of Mac's love as he held her hand. She knew he'd stand by her—no matter what. He'd always be her biggest supporter and cheerleader.

Mac bent over then scooped Lauren into his arms. Over his shoulder, he yelled, "I'm the luckiest man in the world. Mom, please take Todd home. We're off to celebrate." Her carried her out of the classroom toward the parking lot. Catcalls and shouts as well as applause followed them.

Lauren's face felt on fire, was sure her skin appeared beet red from embarrassment.

"Mac, you're my hero. I feel like a princess from a fairy tale. Thank you for defending me and giving me my happily ever after."

The End

ACKNOWLEDGEMENTS

Writers don't create alone. Thank you to my supportive author friends who give me plenty of chances to brag about my books and who enjoy the characters I write. I couldn't do this without your support.

To my family who loves me and understands when I'm unable to do more than grunt at their questions or burn dinner. Your commitment to my happiness is unfathomable.

Finally to my readers, thank you for taking the time to enjoy this story. I'd love to hear from you!

ABOUT THE AUTHOR

As a writer, Melissa likes to keep current on topics of interest in the world of writing. She's a member of the Romance Writers of America and EPIC. Melissa is always interested in improving her writing through classes and seminars. She also believes in helping other authors and features authors and their books on her blog.

Melissa doesn't believe in down time. She's always keeping busy. Melissa is a wife and mother, an elementary school teacher, a book reviewer, co-owner for a publishing company as well as an author. Her home blends two families and is a lot like the Brady Bunch, without Alice—a large grocery bill, tons of dirty dishes and a mound of laundry. She loves to write stories that feature "happy endings" and is often found plotting her next story.

Melissa loves hearing from readers!
www.melissakeir.com
http://www.facebook.com/melissaakeir
http://www.facebook.com/authormelissakeir(fan page)
www.twitter/melissa_keir

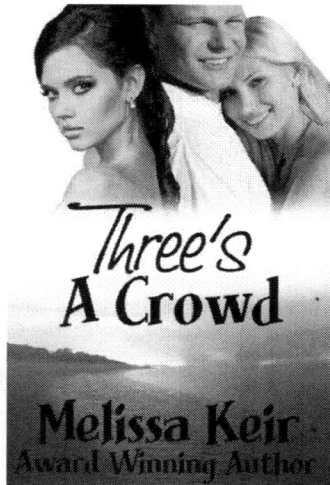

OTHER BOOKS BY MELISSA KEIR

Made in the USA
Columbia, SC
30 June 2017